COME FEED ON ME

COME FEED ON ME

MORTON COOPER

CUTTING EDGE

ISBN-13: 978-1-962896-46-7

Published by
Cutting Edge Books
PO Box 8212
Calabasas, CA 91372
www.cuttingedgebooks.com

CHAPTER ONE

H E SAT AT THE BAR on the fast moving train and watched
the sun-parched fields clattering by the window. He had
been on since Los Angeles, eight long drinks ago. Now the train
was a half hour past Chicago and he was feeling the restlessness
increase in him. He was tired of drinking. He had hoped that
the drinks would kill time, would give him a little glow, but they
weren't helping at all. He wished again that he'd had the sense to
buy more to read than Time and Life.

He shifted his weight on the chrome bar stool and shook
the melted ice in his glass. Damn, he just didn't want another
drink. And besides, he'd run up quite a tab, and he didn't have
an unlimited expense account. He watched the fields, grimly and
vacantly. Then, turning, he nodded to the bartender for another
Scotch and water.

He spread open the copy of Time and turned to the article
again. He'd certainly got his twenty cents' worth. He'd bought
Time without knowing there was a ten-page feature, words and
pictures, on his brother Joe. When he had settled in his chair
at L.A., he'd turned to page eighty-one and found the piece
titled "Joey French, Million-Dollar Dynamo." Now he read
it once more, mesmerized. In the crisp style peculiar to Time,
it told a halfjibing, half-flattering story of the Cinderella boy.
Automatically Al read the opening paragraph again:

Ten years ago ambitious, "Laugh-me-up" Joey French
told bewhiskered gags on second-rate vaudeville stages.

Four years ago he played walk-ons in films, did bits on the Hope, Allen & Berle radio shows. This year, at the age of 36, tall, paunchy, balding French is expected to enrich Treasury coffers and go into direct competition with the U.S. Mint. His TV festival, The Joey French Frolic (Thu. 9-10 EST, R.B.S.), while an insult to intelligence, retains top video rating for the second consecutive year.

Al closed the magazine abruptly and dropped it on a chair a foot away. Let someone else pick the damn thing up. Let someone else turn to the section called "People" and find, instead of Einstein or Bundle or Schweitzer or any guy who was worth a button, the souped-up story of the aging juvenile who'd made good. The truth would be there: the bitter struggle to get to the top, the charitable heart, the three divorces. And the well-meant fiction would be there as well: the "sensitive soul beneath the hard Broadway gloss," "the innate sense of humor, of duty, of compassion," "the genuine friendliness he exudes to cronies and near rivals."

Another drink was placed before him and the sight of it offended him. In that nether region between sobriety and creeping drunkenness, he wished he could show facially how he felt about this drink, about the magazine article, about his reason for being on this train. But in the past year, as if through some dark inner conspiracy, emotion rarely showed on Al French's face. There had been the times when his wife, Louise—dead a year ago Sunday—had stroked his hair and said, "You have the most looking-glass face I've ever seen, darling, did you know that? I think that's why I married you—because of your animation. You can't hide feelings; your face just won't let you."

Funny thing to remember. He smiled slightly, recalling her warmth, her gentleness. Louise had lived in L.A. with him, but her beauty wasn't the contrived movie type, and he had always been proud of that. Had. Before a year ago, when a week-end driver had cut around a corner and run her down, just a block from their apartment. The animation had disappeared from Al French's face after that. He'd stared at walls for a month and he couldn't seem to get his muscles to work. He'd gone back to his disc-jockey spot on KJK, the endless stream of small talk, but his heart felt cluttered inside each time the memory of Louise returned, each time he heard the laughter of a woman.

Facing the window, he heard artificial laughter from one of the tables behind him. When he'd first come into the club car, nine drinks ago, he'd seen only two sailors. Now he turned his head and in the sailors' place he saw a woman and two men. They were all laughing but the woman's laughter was louder, less restrained. She met his eye and her laughter dropped an octave. Al turned back to the window.

She was sitting, slender and straight and expensively dressed, between a pudgy man who was obviously sightless and a tall, blond reed of a man who hung on her words. It occurred to him that her glance indicated recognition. If it did, he would ignore it. Possibly she'd seen him in California, broadcasting from the Villon. Or maybe this was the well-known eye. He grinned. That's a pleasant fantasy, old man, he thought, straight out of Hitchcock. Social-type woman on a train, see, and she's with this odd little blind guy and this futile blond, see, and she takes one look at you and the mountains shake. Cut it out, Alan Arthur French. You're not her kind. You're five feet ten of blank eyes and a once athletic build going to seed. And really, she's not your idea of a dream woman.

"Alan French, isn't it?"

He turned. She was standing at his elbow and her smile was nearly as artificial as her laugh. He looked at her deliberately. She was painfully thin and he felt that if she were to turn her back, he would be able to see the clear outline of her shoulder blades. Facing him, her stern tweed suit outlined very little. Her short black hair didn't quite conceal a strand or two of gray, and her clear face was subtly marked with lines. There was no way now to avoid this encounter, so Al forced a smile of greeting.

"It's Alan French," he said. The blond young man was staring with interest from the table. His blind companion sat hunched over his cane, his mouth slack, his eyes reflecting nothing.

"I'm Margot Connell," the woman announced, and waited expectantly.

"Margot—"

She half sat on the stool next to his and smiled. "My fault. I'm a New Yorker and I expect everyone to light up at my name. But my column doesn't get out to California. Not yet, at any rate."

"Oh, yes," he said. "I'm sorry. Margot Connell. Press-Dispatch, isn't it?"

"That's right. I kept looking at you and looking at you. I was positive I knew you. We got on at Chicago. Let me buy you a drink."

"Thanks, I've—"

"Oh, come on! Your brother and I have been boon companions for years now."

She slid her hand under his arm and guided him to the table. Well, he thought, I've been morose long enough on this trip.

"Mr. French," she said, a possessive hand still on him, "I'd like you to meet my husband, Poppy Colter. And this is Don Haven."

Al extended *a* hand to Colter. Colter brought his hand up, but otherwise stayed still. He was in his late fifties and blindness seemed to have cast an expression of harshness over his pudgy face. "Osborne Colter, isn't it?" Al asked, coming to life.

"Indeed it is," Colter replied, chuckling. His voice was high and soft. "Isn't that lovely, Margot? The gentleman's heard of me."

"Of course I have," Al said, surprised himself that his tone gave the impression of remote hero worship. "I think I've read all your books."

"Delightful! Which one stays with you, Mr. French?"

" 'Normandy Invasion,' I'd say. I can still—"

"Ah, yes. One had nerve in those antediluvian days. An optic nerve, at least."

Margot Connell laughed again, but Al could hear the embarrassment beneath. Her hand directed Al to the other man. Don Haven had a forest of yellow hair, combed in a perfect pompadour, and his chin looked smoother than Margot's. He wore a violent plaid jacket and a foulard ascot. His blue eyes were empty, although he offered a wide tooth-paste grin.

"And this is Don, our precious Don, the constant syncretist," Margot said, and Al accepted his limp handshake. Whatever the hell syncretist meant, Al heard the faint contempt with which it was said.

"Nice to meet you."

"Swell, Alan. Please sit down."

Don moved aside to let Al slide in between him and Margot.

"Well!" Margot exclaimed. "Now we're a happy family. Waiter … Scotch?" She moved her finger in a circle that encompassed all four of them.

"Puss," purred Colter, "tell me: What manner of man is Mr. French?"

She cocked her head. "Oh, quite attractive. Thirty."

"Thanks," Al said. "Thirty-three."

"Thirty-three," she continued. "Firm jaw, not happy. Subject to moods, I'd say."

"Then he hasn't the glowing heroic stature of his eminent brother, mm?" Colter prodded. On the surface it was a harmless enough question, but its effect was needling.

"They're quite different," Margot said.

"But of course." Colter nodded and sat forward an inch. "*This* Mr. French doesn't kiss the girls behind the schoolhouse, does he? Does this Mr. French know about his brother, puss? Does he know Joey is a hero to all the superheal thy young ladies?"

"Please, Poppy," Margot said, uneasiness in her voice.

"Yes, I'm sorry. One doesn't criticize the renowned and obnoxious Joey French. It isn't *de rigeur*, is it, especially in front of his brother."

Al waited, feeling the air heavy with unsaid angers. But then Don cut in and said, tapping long fingers on the table, "I kept screaming we should've flown."

"I know," Margot sighed, "but Poppy just gets terrified if you so much as mention the Wright brothers."

Colter pursed his lips. "That's a groundless lie, but we won't quibble. What does he look like, Margot? Would Buselli have wanted to photograph him?"

Al's shoulders tensed as he felt six eyes, four live and two dead, on him. He would consent to stay on exhibition for a minute more, maybe. Then...

"I don't know what to say, Poppy. Do you mean Buselli before or after he was analyzed? Mr. French has an unusual face; attractive, skirting on depth. There's a sort of stern, determined strength in it. Yes, I'd say Buselli would have clicked his shutter without hesitation."

Don sat forward and lighted Al's cigarette. "Do you know Buselli's work?" he asked, and, not needing an answer, went on. "He did me last year, a month before he died. That was April, just after my concerto was done at Town Hall. He put my picture up with the others at the Metropolitan Museum and it won a prize."

Colter's bloodless lips widened. "April is the cruelest month."

They were talking around each other, to the floor, to the ceiling. He had seen types like these on the Coast and he'd always resented them. How did shallow people get where they had got? How were they able to do a day's work, to create, to persuade audiences into believing that they had sound, sane values? Al knew nothing about Don Haven; but he'd seen too many carbon copies of him, and he knew that Don worked hard to stay a carbon copy. Margot Connell was easy to place, too; she'd had a reputation even ten years ago as a crack journalist. Before that, she'd covered the Hauptmann trial, got some kind of award for it. The last he'd heard of her, a few years back, she'd become movie critic for one of the rowdy, high-circulation tabloids.

But Osborne Colter was difficult. Colter had always been known to be vaguely amoral, nothing serious, but he'd had a power with words that had won him a Nobel and three Pulitzers. He'd been *the* chronicler of the Second World War, starting with the siege of Czechoslovakia, on through D Day, the Japanese surrender, and the Nuremberg Trials. Even when poverty had had Al by the throat, there had always been enough from somewhere to buy a Colter book.

The blindness might have contributed to the superficial frills. But it wasn't the whole reason. It bothered Al and he had to control an urge to ask Colter why he had disintegrated.

"Donald, lad," Colter was saying, "ask the attractive Mr. French if he'd like to make love to my wife."

Margot wheeled on Colter. Her eyes blazed with sudden hate. "What the hell kind of nonsense is that?"

Colter shrugged. "I was only having my fun, puss."

"I asked you: Why did you say such a horrid thing?"

"I merely wanted to see his expression when I said it. Do tell me. How did he take it?"

"Poppy, I've had enough from you. You've been needling me ever since Chicago. I've taken absolutely every kind of—"

Al slid out and dropped a dollar on the bar for his last drink. "Excuse me," he said. "This is too rich for my blood."

He walked past them, past the magazine on the chair opposite, and on out of the car.

He kept on walking, without direction, until suddenly he was in the observation car. He pushed the heavy door forward and went out on the platform. It was growing dark now, he saw, as he first leaned against, then sat, on the side railing. There were clouds that hadn't shown themselves earlier, but which now

showed a milky contrast to the mild blue night. They rolled overhead, threatening, like steel pillows.

He cursed himself mildly for having drunk so much. Then
real anger whipped at him when he remembered that today, at
the age of thirty-three, his bar bill was being picked up by Brother
Joey. This wasn't the way it was supposed to have worked out. Al
was going to have set the world on fire. He wrote music, he wrote
a good lyric, he had the gift of gab. Yessirree, there wouldn't be
any grass growing under ol' Al French. Joey? Well, Joey was
always a good guy in a crowd, a cafeteria comic, a whizbang with
the ladies. But he wouldn't go places. He couldn't add one and
one, and you needed to add to get somewhere. Helluva nice guy,
but write him off as hopeless. Al was the shrewd brother, the one
who'd make the money.

And now here he was, the shrewd brother, using money that
wasn't his own. He had a few hundred dollars in an L.A. bank
and he'd survive as long as he could hang on to the KJK disc-
jockey spot. But he would never have consumed all that liquor
if he'd had to open his own wallet. The realization hurt. He had
managed to make a buck, but there had been the times—Lord,
so many times!—when he'd framed letters in his mind that he
would never send his hopeless brother, letters like "I have a job
but I need money. The breaks don't come my way, no matter
where I turn. You owe me nothing, of course, and all I can think
to say is that you hit it and I didn't. Joe, I'm asking you..." But
there'd always been the last-ditch courage, the refusal to swim in
the foreign sea of prostration, and he had never written.

And then yesterday, the big brother had sent him a hurried
note.

"Al, kiddo," Joey had dictated, "Enclosed please find check
for three notes. Need you, sweetheart. Come right away unless
NBC begs for you. Sorry this must be a rushrush but am tied up
hand and foot with work. Call PL 3-3111 the second you hit town

COME FEED ON ME

and my right-hand boy, Clyde, will be on hand to give directions. Sorry to hear about your missus. Must run now. Love, Joey."

It had been an SOS, Al knew. After ten years Joe needed him for something, and there was nothing to do but run to him.

Short and sweet Joey, he'd always liked to be called. The letter, beyond the call for help, had been the Sunday punch. There was the odor of gloat, which was understandable, because Joe owned the fancy stationery. But the curt condolence, "Sorry to hear about your missus," one year too late, was a slap in the face. Al had needed condolence then. He'd needed help, lots of help. He'd needed money to bury her properly. He'd needed money to get back on his feet. But Joe had been unreachable then. Not at this address. Out to lunch. In rehearsal.

Now, he thought, I'm the boy who comes running when Big Brother beckons. But Joe needs me.

The door was pushed forward and Margot Connell came out on the platform.

"I've been looking for you."

"Got a cigarette?" he asked.

She gave him one, and was silent for a while. Then, "I apologize, Al. I don't condone bad behavior any more than you do."

"Forget it. I'm just jumpy."

"This past week has been dreadful. We were at the Ohlmann Clinic in Chicago for one more checkup. Poppy had so much hope invested in that trip. And it was crushing when they told him."

"I'm sorry."

"His optic nerve is completely severed. There's no chance he'll ever see again. So it wasn't an unusual reaction for him, I suppose, when he heard me describe you, and everything. There must be an exclusive psychology for the blind. The frustration, the jealousy..."

"Yeah. Who's the blond boy?"

"Don? Oh, just someone we know from New York. He was on his way to get a plane ticket when we ran into him, and we persuaded him to wait and take the train with us."

"Mm. Why does your husband hate Joe so much?"

The question, asked quietly, took Margot by surprise. Her hand moved to her throat and she said, "Hate?"

"He was just a needier with everything else. But he hates Joe's guts. His tone gave him away. What's he got against him?"

"I ... don't know. I don't think there's—any real — I—"

"O.K., forget it."

She relaxed. "All right. Let's."

"And do you mind, Margot? I'd like to be by myself."

She came to the front of the rail and stood there, letting the wind brush gently against her close-cropped hair. She gave no indication that she had heard him.

"I'm glad you're going to see Joey, Al."

His eyes widened. "You know everything, don't you?"

"I know Joey very well. We all do, and we love him. I've been a bit more intuitive, maybe, than the others. I know, for instance, he's toting a torch for Lory Kimball. You know, that girl in 'Cloud Number Seven.' Or maybe you don't. Anyway, perhaps that's his reason for writing you to come to New York—to ask your advice about her. He's told me dozens of times that you know everything in the world."

"How do you know he wrote me?"

"I told you. I know Joey very well. I figured the rest."

"Look, Miss Connell or Mrs. Colter or whatever you call yourself. I don't condone your behavior any more than theirs. I like people to talk to me, not somewhere between my toes or over my head. What 'rest' did you figure? Talk or go back inside, will you?"

She laughed softly. "You're as emotional as Joey. Different, though, of course. I'll go back in."

"Excuse me. Lately I've got out of the habit of talking to people."

"I'll see you, you know. I'm usually not far from Joey."

"O.K., O.K."

"He wrote you because he needs help. He's in trouble. He thinks he can rely on others, but apparently you're the only one he trusts. Help him, Al."

"What kind of trouble?"

"I'm going in; it's chilly. Just don't go to him for favors, that's all I'm saying. If you can help him, help him. Good-by, Al," she said, and went in.

At a quarter past midnight Lory Kimball descended the short flight of carpeted stairs that led to the mammoth living room. Within the past few minutes she had sobered—magically, it seemed. She saw the bar at the far end of the room and recalled that she had been instructed to fix two drinks there. She started for it.

It was an expensively furnished room and its tastefulness surprised her. She had been attracted to Joey French the week before at Mitch's party and this evening she had agreed to come here for the veiled but certain purpose of being more attracted to him. And somehow she had convinced herself that she would find his apartment stuffed with Kewpie dolls and gaudy pincushions. He had impressed her as a totally uncivilized man, almost apelike, but, she thought now, that had been her lone reason for coming—his primitive charm.

In the car, on the way over, it had all seemed so right, though a little cold-blooded. Lory Kimball, the girl who chose her men with care, had agreed to join Joey French simply because he stirred her physically. But now— Why do I ever take more than one drink when I know I'm just not cut out to drink? Now she wanted to leave.

She stopped at the table near the couch and found a cigarette. Joey French, the clown. Joey French, who'd told her he'd had a haircut just that afternoon but who still needed a shave.

There was stubble on his chin and he was upstairs now, deciding whether to shave or put talcum on his face. Joey French.

At the bar Lory looked at the stock of bottles. With methodical speed she prepared two bourbons and soda. She reached for one and sat on the bar stool. She sipped from it with a kind of gentle desperation, but the taste of the whisky depressed her, and she set the glass down.

This is preposterous, she told herself. I've never been comfortable in leering men's apartments. I'm twenty-six and suddenly I find myself an adventuress. I'm not a tart, I've never been a tart. I'm Lory Kimball, the bird-brain actress, and in just nine months I've been glorified in Life, Collier's, Look, and, God save us, Theatre Arts. I just finished paying more income tax than I earned in all the fiscal years between 1945 and 1952. So what in the name of heaven am I doing in Joey French's elegant apartment—or *any* strange man's apartment?

"Honey?"

The harsh rasp from the stairs frightened her out of her glum investigation. She sat forward. The voice, the deep and masculine timbre, suddenly shook and excited her.

"Yes?"

"I shaved."

Nothing circled in Lory's head until she closed her eyes, and then she felt sick.

The bourbon burned her stomach. A cold anxiety stumbled awkwardly through, cutting across the heat of the liquor, and she knew he had come into the room.

Joey French came toward her.

"I wasn't long, was I?" He was a giant of a man, even with those stooped shoulders. Earlier, she recalled, he had looked at her very gravely in the back seat of his chauffeur-driven car and told her she wasn't just a dame to him, by God, she was something very special. And she had liked him. But now—particularly now, with this standard-brand, expectant smile he was offering—everything was wrong. She had been told that he was a darn nice fellow and that many people loved him; maybe that had impressed her. His reputation as a television clown hadn't warmed her, certainly. She had tuned in his show some months back for the first time, and clicked it off within minutes. She had told somebody at the time, "I can't seem to get used to this art form. I can watch the dance, the film, the drama, any of the lively arts, but not pie-throwing."

"You look sleepy, honey," he was saying now. "What's wrong? Half hour ago you had the energy o' ten men."

She smiled and asked him some questions she cared nothing about. She needed time to think. And as he talked and looked at her without subtlety, she concentrated on the hours lost between the time she'd agreed to come here and now. Now, when she knew quite well that she wasn't going to be compliant for *this* adolescent monster. He was one of the bright headlights of the entertainment world, she'd been told. He made children laugh. She had been in Montmartre and she had seen a clown named Bobo who made children laugh. Bobo had wiggled his ears and fallen on his face, not with one eye on the sponsor's approval, but majestically. The children had laughed, with their eyes and their hearts. Bobo washed dishes in a café and Bobo died penniless.

"Like I say, honey, I got a talent for yakety-yak, they tell me. You know how people say. But now I'm damn near speechless. I saw you an' I said, 'This is it.' But for real, ya know? Honey, what I'm tryna bring out is I really like you a whole lot."

She looked at him and everything about him was offensive and vulgar to her. This was an oaf raised up as a god on the shoulders of tiny half gods, this was a man with patented charm and personality.

He moved closer and kissed her. When he finished, disappointment clouded his face.

"What happened?"

She met his eyes. "What happened? You kissed me."

"What's a matter? You fall asleep?"

"Not at all. I've got the energy of ten men. Someone told me that once."

"In the car you were different."

"Was I? I guess I was." She smiled for him.

"I don't get it. What's the idea of the iceberg routine?"

"I just remembered. I've got to go."

He stepped back. "Go? What kind a—"

"Pressing business, Mr. French. Will you please lower the drawbridge and let me pass?"

She walked stiffly out of the living room to a hall chair where her purse and jacket lay. She glanced at herself in one of the mirrors. She was aware that she needed lipstick, but she could not stay in this apartment any longer. She could not stay with him.

He stood in front of the door.

"Is this one of your comedy sketches, too?" she asked without anger.

"I wanna know how come you changed your mind, all of a sudden."

"Mr. French, someone should have told you that I'm the easiest girl in the world to invite for a drink. But when someone wants to paw me, I yell loud enough to bring in the neighbors. Now stand aside."

"O.K., you don't hafta get tough. We'll have a drink and talk. What's that hurt? C'mon. I told you I like you."

She unlocked the door and found herself in a private vestibule. She pressed the elevator button.

"Ja hear me? We'll forgive an' forget."

"Thanks. I'm really not a very nice girl, Mr. French. Thanks for the drink."

"I'll have the guy drive you home."

"No."

"Honest, I don't know how come, out of a blue sky—"

"I know. It's my fault, not yours. Please excuse me." The elevator door opened and she stepped in. "Good night."

He listened for a while to the car descending. Didn't she believe him when he told her he was on the level, that he really liked her? She was class. That's what he was trying to explain to her. Couldn't she see he really liked her?

He returned to the apartment and bolted the door. He was alone. He walked from room to room, switching on every light in every room. He glanced at his watch. Not even one o'clock yet. And he was alone. For a moment he stood irresolute, then he went to his desk in the den. He opened his address book and raced through the pages. Finger on a number, he dialed it so frantically he fumbled. He cursed and dialed again. When Nora answered he brought himself up to his full, assured strength and asked if the party was still going. Nora said, "Sure, man, just beginning!" He promised to be there in thirty minutes.

He hurried to the bedroom, throwing off his robe as he went. Suddenly he remembered Al, remembered Al's wire. Al would be in town in an hour or so. He picked up the bedroom phone and dialed the answering service. He gave the girl Nora's number and cautioned her to give it only to Mr. Alan French.

He dressed rapidly in the new $230 Brooks Brothers brown suit. He faced himself in the mirror. He studied the huge, friendly face, the strength, the determined brown eyes.

What was wrong? Didn't she know he really went for her, that she was something different to him? Didn't she know they did a ten-page spread on him in Time, for God's sake, the same magazine where they write up the Queen of England and the President of the United States, for God's sake?

Didn't she know he was Joey French?

Outside, the night was wonderfully fresh. Lory walked without direction, her eyes caressing the sight of New York after midnight. The breezes were quiet and the air soft with cool fragrance.

She discovered herself near the Hudson River and she moved closer to watch it. So it had happened again, she thought. So many times she had been drawn to attractive men, convinced that each new relationship might be the right one. But at the crucial moments the attractive men had turned into ogres, like Joey French. It was her own fault, she knew, for starting things she couldn't finish. But somewhere there had to be a man with whom she could sustain interest, the right man, the man who would be kind and gentle and complete....

CHAPTER TWO

A L PHONED from a Grand Central booth. The answering service gave him Nora's number. He called there.

"Yeah," a woman said abruptly. He could hear music and raucous noises beyond her.

" Joey French, please. This is his brother."

She was guarded. "Brother?"

Al inhaled wearily. "Brother," he said. "Mr. French's brother."

He heard a short exchange on the other end, a booming voice, and then Joe. "Hey, there, ya mutt!"

Al yanked the receiver away from his ear. "Hello, Joey. Keep it down to a yell, will you?"

"How you doin', sweetheart? Just land?"

"Few minutes ago. You sound fine, Joe."

"Let's see. Quarter of two now. Ya got a pencil? Wanna write this address down?"

"I'll tell you, Joe. I'm knocked out from the trip. I'd like to get into a tub and relax."

"What are ya, a hunnert years old? I haven't slept moren' eight hours in the past week an' I'm havin' a ball, kid. Take this address down." He gave a street number in the West Eighties with detailed instructions. It was a basement flat, go down, keep straight, an' you'll see this little arrow. "Check your bags at the station and bring along the key. I'll send the boy down for them later. Ya got the story, Al? Snap it up."

Exhausted, frustrated, Al took his suitcase to a locker and deposited it. He headed for a cab stand but thought the hell with it, he hadn't been in New York for ten years now and it would be a kick to ride a subway, tired as he was. He bought a Times and a Tribune and remembered to take a shuttle to Times Square.

He read Joey's name three times. The Trib reported that Joey had signed a contract with Gilford Pictures for a single-picture deal. The Times printed an arm-long list of celebrities who were to take part in a Madison Square Garden benefit in a few weeks. Joey French was to M.C.

On another page Al saw the Times headline: "Joey French Gives $10,000 to Heart Fund." He read the article with interest. Joey was a member of The Gang, a fraternal organization for men in the theatrical business. Each member had made a good contribution, but none had equaled Joey's. That was Joey, Al thought; even in the struggle days he never turned down a plea for a buck. He might have overlooked Al and the other relatives, but he'd always been up there when it came to contributions to good causes.

Al's feelings gradually warmed toward Joe and he reconsidered this trip to New York. Maybe things would turn out well, after all. Maybe he could shrug this personal chip off his shoulder and come alive again. He was almost glad he'd come, now.

He glanced up sharply when the train stopped. He'd planned to get off at 86th Street. The sign outside read 103rd Street. Oh, great! he thought, and jumped up. And I'm the guy who knows this town like a book.

He climbed to the street and hailed a cab. He looked at his watch. Two-thirty-five. He desperately wanted a bath and a bed. His clothes were rumpled and he needed a shave. Maybe he should have warned Joe that he looked so frayed. The hell with it. He wasn't out to impress anyone. Joe was the actor in the family.

He glanced at the cabbie's card. It read Clifford Demioski.

"Cliff?" he said.

"Yeah."

"You ever see Joey French on television?"

"Yeah, I've caught 'im."

"I'm just in from out of town. I've heard a lot about him. What's your opinion?"

"Me, personally, he's good for a laugh. The wife an' kid're nuts about him. The kids especially."

"He makes a lot of money, they say. You think he's worth it?"

Cliff shrugged. "Listen, it's like I tell the wife. We make a man like that, we build 'im up, we watch 'im. No, I don't think he's worth all that dough. But I drive a hack twelve, fourteen hours a day. Maybe if I could tell jokes, make that kinda dough, maybe I'd change my tune. Hell, I know I would."

Al got out on Central Park West, and walked down half a block till he saw the number 17. He started for the basement. A man materialized from the shadow of the next building and followed him. Al stopped and turned around. The other stopped too.

This was no mugger, Al was convinced. The man was small and wan, fifty-five, sixty tops. It was early September but he wore an overcoat, a threadbare tweed, and the brim of his battered hat hid his forehead.

Al took another step down. The man came forward, his face worried and drawn, hands in his pockets.

"Where are you going?" His voice was hesitant.

"Downstairs. Where are *you* going?"

The man advanced. "You going to that harlot's place?"

Al frowned. "What do you want, mister?"

"My little girl's down there. They got my little girl down there. You going down there, too?"

"Wait a minute. Who's got your girl down there?"

"That actor. That television actor, France. Joe France. He got my baby. Mister, I—" The man's mouth jerked in pain. "Mister, she's all I got, my little Virginia. Since her mother passed away, she's all I got. Just eighteen, she is. And they won't even let me in. They say go away, she ain't in there, they never heard of her, that's how they lie to me, that's how they talk."

"Look, Mr.—"

"Hutch."

"Mr. Hutch, you wait here."

Al followed directions to Nora's door, and knocked once. Mr. Hutch appeared behind him.

A woman's voice, the one he'd heard on the phone, said, "Yeah?"

"Al French."

A peephole in the door opened quietly, speak easy fashion, and one eye raced up and down, inspecting Al. He heard the sound of caged music and excited voices. The peephole clicked down and the door swung open.

Nora wore a taffy-colored blouse and shapeless blue jeans. Her mouth widened and she said huskily, "Fall in, man!" Al moved forward, half looking behind him. Then Mr. Hutch, trembling now, tried to push in after Al, but Nora's arm barred the way.

She showed no anger, only impatience. "Come on, Pops, whaddaya say? Beat it."

"Let me in!"

"Look, Pops. How many times I gotta lay it on you? Whoever your daughter is, she isn't here!"

Al turned to the front room, his curiosity aroused. In that instant Joey appeared, peering around the partly closed inner door, a shadow of concern on his face. He disappeared suddenly and a few of the people there stopped their talk to watch his exit. An animal roar went up from Nora and when Al turned back he saw that Hutch had stormed inside.

"She's here!" Hutch cried. "She's here an' I'll take her home, away from this iniquity!" And he broke into the front room. Nora shot a glance at Al as they both followed.

Hutch stood in the center of a room that was filled with a bed, a piano, table, chairs, and bar stools without seeming crowded. Al's eyes raced to find Joey, but he had gone, apparently with the girl, for Hutch's frustration heightened now in a spasm of tears. There was a small window in the opposite wall, above the bed, but it led to blackness and Al could see nothing beyond it.

"Where is she?" Hutch whispered. He clenched his fists at his sides. "Out that window! They went out there!"

For a moment he rocked on his heels, still weeping, and his bitter incoherencies were out of place in the gaudy room.

"Let 'im get it out," someone ordered. "Don't never drag a cat when he's bawling, don't matter what he's done."

Al studied the room and counted eleven people, more than half of them women. What appeared to be a music session—a stern, heavy-set girl was at the piano and Nora came to stand near a set of drums—had dwindled away since Hutch's entrance. A couple on the bed moved restively, their eyes on the rocking father. A clear-eyed red-head, who looked like a Westchester matron, held her drink a few inches from her lips, seemingly sensitive to Hutch's pain. The others had recovered, talking, urging the girls on with the music, drinking, ignoring the entire disturbance.

Al moved to Hutch and put a hand on his shoulder. "Maybe it's best to go home, Mr. Hutch. Where do you live?"

The man looked at him vacantly. "Queens."

"Then get a subway and go home to bed. Things'll work out."

"I want my girl."

"She'll be all right. She isn't here. Maybe she's home now, herself."

"She's with that actor."

"Go home, Mr. Hutch. Get some sleep. Things'll be O.K." He guided him to the door. "Don't worry. Go on home now. Everything'll work out."

When the door closed behind Hutch and Al returned, the frantic noise welled up again—piano, drums, and clinking ice. The Westchester redhead went to a full-length mirror near Al and called, "School's over, Gin!" then moved the mirror to one side. A door opened behind it and a girl emerged from the small hidden room, smiling like a triumphant child.

She came directly to Al, wrapped in a man's woolen robe. She rubbed her face against his shoulder and giggled. "You're a doll." She was hardly different from the scores of ingénues he'd seen on the Coast: commercially attractive, overpainted, trying always to hold in her stomach and her fear of the nameless terrors. Nice-looking kid, Al thought, but what kind of fool is Joey that he'd risk his fame for dollar-a-dozen stuff like this?

"Everybody," she announced, "let me introduce my white knight, Al French!" Some of them applauded. There was a sweet quality to her voice that blurred the picture of a slightly tight teen-ager. "Joey wants all of you to give Al the keys to the city!"

"Where is Joe?" he asked.

Virginia laughed. "He cut out."

Nora's eyebrows lifted. "How fussy can he get? Why'd he cut out?"

"You know," Virginia said. "Nervous in the service. C'mon, Al. We gotta cut, too. Joey's expecting us. Wait here, have a drink. I'll be right back." She disappeared into the other room.

The bop picked up and Al leaned against a miniature bureau, wishing he had the guts to leave, to take a room for the night, to stay clear of Joe and all the messed-up people who surrounded Joe.

Idly he watched Nora bound up again from her chair and move past him to the front door. He heard her say, "Yeah," and, in a second, open the door. "Hey, baby!" she roared in delight, and came back hand in hand with Don Haven.

The crowd greeted him. "Hi, Don!" "Lookooz here!" "Honey!" A clatter of talk fanned up and Al's stomach gnawed in anger. He turned away. He didn't want to see Haven and, for some obscure reason, he didn't want Haven to see him.

He moved the mirror and went into the other room. Virginia was being lectured about something by a boy with glazed eyes who crouched on a day bed, a brownpapered cigarette hanging from his lips. They looked up as Al came in. "Did Joe go out this way?" Al pointed to still another door.

Virginia nodded. "Leads to Eighty-fifth."

"Ready? Let's go."

He put his hand on the doorknob. The girl, sensing his urgency, picked up an orange jacket and said, "Dig ya, Steve."

The boy brought his hand up and blinked, trying to keep smoke out of his eyes. "Dig ya, Gin."

The doorway faced a twisting, squalid alley and Al saw no light leading to the street. "You say this is Eighty-fifth?"

She took his hand. "Doll, where's your faith?" She led him through the darkness, sure of herself. The alley smell merged somehow with her strong perfume and her tight grip shot an involuntary excitement through him.

They walked a distance and soon they came to the corner of Columbus Avenue and West 85th. "This means extra steps for us," she told him, "but chances are Pop's still hugging the lamp-post in front of Nora's. C'mon, there's a cab."

They ran and her heels made crisp tapping sounds on the pavement. They caught the cruising taxi on Columbus Avenue and startled the driver with their sudden appearance.

They got in and Virginia gave a Lexington Avenue address. Once the cab started she sat back, took Al's hand, and faced him. "Hi." She grinned. "I'm Virginia."

CHAPTER THREE

S ITTING BACK and away from her, Al revised his original esti-
mate. He'd been told she was eighteen, and even in the smoky
glitter of Nora's place she'd looked eighteen. But he thought
now of his sister-in-law in California, Louise's kid sister, Emily.
He'd seen her just three or four months ago and she'd gently
reminded him that she was celebrating her eighteenth birthday
that evening. Emily was a freshman at UCLA, hoping to major
in biochemistry. And, despite the teen-age speech affectations,
she had what Al considered the typical eighteen-year-old expression: eyes bright, with the wonderful love of life, the energy, the
inquisitive, intelligent mind. Virginia Hutch, brassy, wise, and
imitative, resembled nothing of Emily or her age.

"What're you so *glum* about, Al?" she was asking. She brushed
her palm against his cheek. "You're positively dour, doll! C'mon,
cheer up. Don't tell me Joey has all the spark in the family."

"Seems he does."

Virginia pulled a cigarette from her pocket and had already
struck a match before Al recognized the brown paper. He yanked
it from her mouth.

"Hey!"

"Screwball," he muttered. He broke it in half and stuffed it
in his pocket.

She stared at him angrily. "Al, I wanna tell you. You're beginning to drag me."

"Relax, Virginia. There's nothing more you have to prove to
me."

"What's that mean?"

"I believe you're twenty-one and all grown up."

She paused, as though deciding whether to continue the duel. Then she laughed and looked at him from beneath her eyelashes. "You're sharp, you know that?"

Al offered her a Chesterfield. "How far is Joe's place from here? Why didn't he wait?"

She didn't seem to hear. "Joey told me a dozen times about you, said you're the smartest guy on two legs. Said you played records for the squares on the Coast."

"Not so square."

"I dig a sharp guy, Al. I dig a cat's intellect, y'know? I couldn't dig a fella if he didn't have something upstairs."

"O.K. Why didn't Joe wait?"

"Joey's sharp, too. In a different way than you, but he digs everything in life. Everybody talks like how he's a comic twenty-four hours a day and how he doesn't have his serious side. But he and I, we were walking last night and we passed this ash can near the gutter and you know on top of that can we saw a cat. She was dead."

Virginia looked off through the window. "Poor cat, had a grin on her face. I got kinda scared a little. That isn't the happiest thing to look at when you don't expect it, but you should've dug Joe. He went white. He starts shakin' a little, his shoulders going back and forth like he's crying inside himself, you know? That's something to see, a man six feet two and three-quarters inches tall, nervous like that. Did you ever see him that way? I just couldn't pull him out of it. He didn't say a word, but oh, a couple hours later, I looked at him and he was still sort of depressed, like, and I says, 'Honey, is it on account of that cat in the ash can, dead?' And he looks at me and he nods, and he says. 'Yeah, it sort of takes the starch out of you, you know?' Just like that. Can you imagine, from seein' a dead cat?"

"Why didn't Joe wait?" Al insisted.

"Oh, that. Joey's always like that. Something inside of him, he can't stand still for two minutes. On the go every two minutes. Very excitable fella. Herb had the car waitin' for him and he just said to get you when the coast was clear and bring you home."

Al studied her. She liked to talk, that was evident, with the effect of sophistication. When her voice and manner reverted to eighteen years, though, she would remember it and leap back to the impersonation of maturity.

He decided to try her guard. "When what coast was clear?"

"Oh, *you* know."

"Know what?"

"My faw-ther."

"Tell me, Virginia, is the old man as square as that?"

"Square?"

"Is he a corn ball?"

"Nobody said he was."

"What do you feel about him?"

She moved away from Al, thought a minute, then shrugged her shoulders. "Oh, if you like that kind of a man."

"That's a pretty sophisticated answer."

Virginia was pleased. "Was it?"

"Maybe a little *too* jaded, though. What's wrong with him?"

"Let's talk about something else. Did you know Joey had me do a spot on his show last week?"

"I'd rather talk about you and your father."

"What are you, one of those psychiatrists or something?"

"No. I'd like to see you stay on the ball, though."

"What do you call doing a spot on the Joey French show before I'm even nineteen? That's on the ball. Don't preach me a sermon, please."

"I'll tell you something, Virginia. Maybe it'd be smart to get out and go back to Queens."

"Man, you're fiippin'!" She crossed her legs and tucked her skirt over her knees.

"I might be." He nodded. "But in the long run you'll want to come to some understanding with him. He's not necessarily right, but you're not necessarily right, either."

"Will you please take off that record?"

"Try it on your own, Virginia. Try to make the top without reefers and talking like a bad imitation of Thelonius Monk. Don't toss that cute shape around like it was public property."

She grinned. "You really think it's cute?"

Al slouched. "I give up," he said, feeling like a defeated social worker.

"Don't, Al. I'm not mad. I like to listen to you."

"Yeah."

"I do. You're so funny. You sound like a judge or a mortician or something, putting on an act. I don't mind, honest. Joey warned me you'd be a very serious type, so I was prepared."

She snuggled close to him, her forehead under his chin.

When the cab stopped, Al drew his wallet from his pocket, but Virginia, climbing over his legs, had already placed two bills in the driver's hand. "Doctor's orders," she told Al. Her fingers dug into his arm and she jerked him toward the oversized lobby.

She offered a patronizing "Hiya, Ernie," to the elevator operator, but he gave no indication that he had heard her. Virginia, undaunted, wriggled excitedly all the way up to the seventeenth floor. The elevator was richly carpeted and Al couldn't help thinking of the six rickety flights of stairs the Frenches had climbed daily years ago in Newark.

Ernie opened the door to let them out into the private vestibule. Virginia appeared to remember only then that she had a door key. Again Al felt helpless as he waited. She rummaged through the pockets of her orange coat, aware of his attention, and reveling in it. Finally she unlocked the door and led him into a fully lighted apartment. "Joey's home. If it looks like a benefit for the light company, that means Joey's home." She dropped her jacket on the hall chair and beckoned him into the living room.

As he walked, Al felt surprised at the taste, the simplicity, the sense of unassuming wealth. This didn't look like Joe. Not Joe the back-slapper, who had approved of nothing in the Newark days unless it had color and plenty of it. Al had never been able to form a mental picture of Joe without adding the suede shoes, the gaudy jackets, the hand-painted ties.

A wiry young man in a chauffeur's uniform was sitting alone on the living-room sofa. He took his eyes from his tabloid only long enough to look at them. Then he turned a page and went on reading.

"Herb," Virginia said, affecting a *grande dame* air, "where's Mr. French at?"

"In his study," Herb replied. "Wants me to take a locker key, go down to the station, and pick up a bag." He made no motion to rise.

"Got the key, Al?" Virginia asked. Al nodded and took it from his pocket. He tossed it lightly for a moment, until Herb folded his paper, jammed it down the back pocket of his trousers, and came to them. He did not look directly at either of them. He reminded Al of all the young tenors he'd seen at burlesque shows.

Taking the key, Herb started for the living-room landing. He said to Virginia over a shoulder, "Mr. French says to make some drinks. He'll be out soon."

"Who's with him? Clyde?"

"Yeah." Herb left, slamming the front door shut.

"Brr-rr." Virginia laughed and went to the bar at the other end of the room.

"That Herb," Al remarked, following Virginia, who seemed to know her way around the bar. "Is he always that surly?"

"What's surly?"

"He didn't act very happy."

"Oh, that. He's the biggest pain there is. I told Joey a dozen times he ought to kick him out."

Al glanced at his watch. "It's almost four in the morning. Does Herb work around the clock?"

Busy dropping ice in two large glasses, Virginia kicked her shoes off. One went winging onto the sofa. "Oh, any time Joey wants him. It's like everybody who works for Joey. They're mostly all so dumb they couldn't make twenty-five a week anywheres else. But Joey pays them all this money just so's he'll have them any time he wants them. Like Clyde, that's his right-hand guy, does everything for Joey. He's around any time Joey calls him. But most of 'em are dumb wops, like."

Al sat at the bar stool farthest from her. Stupid kid with a pretty face, Al thought, unable to work up any real anger toward her. The pretty face, looking up at the stars, at the rigid mold called fame. Going to get to the top because she's eighteen and positive she has the only enticing body in the world.

"You're quite a bitter young lady, Virginia."

"You're draggin' me again, Al."

"I apologize."

"I've got one theory about all that stuff. I've been on television and Joey's putting me in his picture next summer and he's promised me he'll get me other jobs, too. By the time I'm twenty-one I'll have more money'n I know what to do with. That's all that counts in life. I'm gonna be a star. I can say any damn thing to anybody I want to."

"Does Joey agree with this intellectual eloquence?"

"Joey never thinks anything. He's too busy being smart, making his loot, and keeping his name before the public."

"A public that includes wops?"

Virginia banged a glass on the counter. "Shut up, you! Who're you to talk to me like that? I know all about you, you and your hifalutin holy-rollin'. You got ten cents to your name, huh?"

"Calm down, Modjeska."

"When you got money in the satchel and they put your picture in the paper, *then* you can come and talk to me like you know all the answers. Don't you give me any of that, mister. Even today I could buy you and sell you."

And, as quickly as it had flared, her hate disappeared. She returned to the drinks. Her pretty mouth eased and she produced a winning smile.

"Al, there's one thing you've got to learn so's we'll all get along friendly. I'm Joey's girl. He had a big write-up in Whatsaname Magazine this week and the whole world takes off their hat to him. What he says goes and he says I'm his girl. So let's all be friendly, O.K.? I hate for everybody to be sore."

"How long have you two known each other?"

"Long enough. I might even marry him."

"Well. Good for you."

Virginia handed him a drink with too much ice and too much whisky. She clutched her glass and went to the phonograph. "You dig Bird Parker?" she asked rhetorically. She flipped a switch and Al recognized Parker's horn immediately. The music acted as a challenge to Virginia. "Dance, Al?" He shook his head. He leaned against the bar and watched her move around the room, interpreting freely, her eyes closed, her expression happy. From time to time she sipped at her drink.

When she asked him later if he'd like another drink, he refused. She mixed a fresh one for herself, and Al watched, yawning. It was nearly an hour before Joey appeared. When he clattered into the room Al had fallen asleep on the couch, and Virginia was quarrelsomely drunk.

"Hey!" Joe cried, slapping Al's leg. "I turn my back for two seconds an' everybody saws wood! How are ya, you beautiful mutt?"

Al roused himself, a part of his mind still clinging to a forgotten dream. Joe was tousling his hair with fierce affection.

"Hello, Joe," Al said sheepishly. "Must've dozed off for a minute."

Joe reached for the phonograph and lifted the arm. "Damn nutty kid." He grinned. "I got the joint sound-proofed, but it sounds like you could hear it in Newark."

There was no doubting Joe's authority, Al thought as he stretched his arms. He stalks around as if he could move mountains. Probably could, too. Al looked at his watch again. "My God, it's nearly five o'clock!"

Joey returned to Al, stopping at the bar long enough to pull Virginia's skirt down over her knees. She was lying on three of the four bar stools and staring at nothing in particular.

"What you been doin', Al?" Joey asked, and sat heavily beside him. "Sousin' up my sweetie? Lemme look at you, ya gorgeous mutt! Hey, Gin, you sober enough to fix me a ginger ale?"

Virginia glared at him, but rose and went behind the bar. "So I asked ya," Joey bellowed, slapping Al's thigh. "Whaddaya been doin' these days?"

"I've been chasing a maniacal brother around Manhattan."

Joe's huge head shot back and he roared. "Still the kidder! You mean the Nora deal. I just didn't wanna get in a hassel with the old guy. Sorry I'm late here. I came home an' Clyde wanted to give me the lowdown on the schedule for the week. Couple letters, that stuff. Say, you're a sight for sore eyes. Never saw you lookin' so good."

Virginia brought the glass to Joe.

"Don't I get a kiss?" she asked, blinking drowsily.

Joe ignored her. "Bet you wonder how anything gets done around here, Al. That creep from Time was here, he couldn't figure out how I worked. I'm always movin', ya know? I got thirty-seven people on the payroll just to keep me in line. Did you know that? But it gets done. Somehow nothin' gets overlooked."

"Say," Virginia called shrilly, "what am I aroun' here, fifth wheel onna wagon or somp'm? I'm Virginia, remember?"

Joe bounded from the sofa and crooked his finger for Al to get up. "C'mon, kid. Follow the leader." He dropped his strong hands to Virginia's shoulders and kissed her ear. "What's a matter, baby, you feelin' rejected? Give Al and me a little while an' then we'll live, O.K.?" Virginia pouted. As Al watched, Joey kissed her with unexpected tenderness. Her sulkiness changed instantly to the exuberance Al had witnessed earlier.

"All you needed was a little wake-up medicine, see?" Joey laughed and released her. He stalked out of the living room, Al following tiredly behind.

As he moved, Joey unbuttoned his shirt and dropped it to the carpet. He continued to undress as he walked, dropping clothes from room to room, so that he left a zigzag trail. By the time they arrived at the bathroom Joe was nearly ready for the tub, which was full and fragrant with cologne. Little clouds of steam rose from the water as Joey stepped in. "Everything around here's mechanized. Herb came back, put your stuff in your room, and fixed the bath for me. Minute doesn't get wasted around here, ya know?"

Al pointed to the water. "Who's your sponsor this year? Chanel?"

"Hey! Ya kill me. How do ya like the smell? Sometimes I think. I'm part queer, the way I go for this stuff. But ten minutes in here before I hit the sack an' the tenseness eases out."

He began muscle exercises then, raising, lowering, extending his arms, feeling their weight. "Whatta you starin' at, Al? I been talkin'."

Al shook his head and grinned. "All this finery, Joe. I'm impressed."

Joey roared. "Damn right! Way you stare, though, you look like you're just in from the sticks. Come on, kiddo! If you're gonna be my number-one boy, you gotta act the part an' act it big."

"Number-one boy?"

"It all figures, baby. That's why I sent you the smoke signal to come on back. I can't trust any of these muzzlers hangin' around. With you, you're flesh an' blood, you appreciate good living, you got class. I can trust ya, ya know what I mean? So I'll slap five hundred in your shoe every week, so you'll look out for me. So I take it off the income tax an' we keep it in the family."

"Five hundred? That's a lot of—"

Joey looked at him fully for the first time since he'd got in the tub. "Don't talk like a farmer, baby. A hundred G's is big money. Five hundred's no money. That's the way it goes around Joey French. You're gonna really live, kid."

"What do I do for five hundred a week?"

Joey frowned and squeezed a sponge that sent water cascading over his head. "What kinda question is that?"

"Serious question, Joe. I never heard a toot from you when I was really on my can. Why the gold rush now?"

"I told ya, fa Pete's sakes, if you'd only listen to a guy! You'll look out for me, let a little class rub off once in a while. I slip Clyde two-fifty an' he's not working out. So I double it for you and—"

"You mean I'll be your secretary?"

Joey sat up. His expression was half quizzical, half amused. "You're off your nut, boy. You're talkin' like the parish priest. Whadda ya think I called ya out for? I got a lot of trouble, stuff runnin' around in the head. I can't go to strangers for help, so I look to my own."

"Trouble?"

"Awright, now's no time to gas around. Tomorrow's another day. Listen, mize well change the tune an' give ya some good news. I met a chick, Al, a chick like you never see except you're dreamin'. You ever hear of Lory Kimball?"

Al nodded. "Quite a girl. She's doing a show now, isn't she? I read about her on the Coast."

"The same. She's makin' a nothing out of Geraldine Page, Julie Harris, all of 'em. I'm not sayin' it's in the bag yet, but I've been flippin' my cork since I met her. She's gonna be the next Mrs. French, I don't care if I have to clap her over the head."

Al pointed to the door. "What about our sweet little Virginia?"

Joey slouched, snorting. "Ahh, that don't mean a thing. Just a kid. I'm gonna kick her home in a couple days."

"Look, Joe. I hear I've got a reputation for being a preacher, but there's one thing that stands out in these few crazy hours I've been in town. You've done enough tonight alone, involving yourself with that kid, to get you sent up to stripe college till everyone forgets there *was* a Joey French."

The corners of Joey's mouth turned downward and for a moment he seemed reflective. Then he said, "I can't argue with you, doll. Things get in me sometimes, an' I blow my top. But it'll work out. Hell, everything's worked out so far."

Al was about to answer when he heard a timid scratching of nails. Both men looked at the door.

"Yeah?" Joey called.

"Guess who?"

"Come in," Joey laughed, and shrugged. "Dizzy kid," he whispered.

Virginia wore a white silk robe, obviously Joey's, and her small body seemed lost in it. Her hair was loose over her shoulders, drifting as she moved.

"Who told you you could disturb our conference?" Joe asked with affection.

"I got real restless, honey."

"You hear that, Al?" Joe laughed. "The kid's restless."

As though posing for a photograph, she leaned against the doorjamb for a moment. Her leg showed through the robe.

Al got up. "Pardon me, folks," he said, and went out of the room.

He looked into three lighted bedrooms before he found his suitcase. A little door near the bed led to a shower. He undressed and stood beneath a hot spray, trying to keep his mind empty.

Maybe I'm the fishhead, he told himself. Maybe I'm the one who's out of step. Alan Arthur French, the shrewd boy who was always only a quarter inch from everything he wanted. Why am I acting like the head of the Vice Squad? Nobody kidnaped me to bring me here. I came with my hat very soberly in hand, ready to accept any bone. Stop the moralizing, French. It's like what the cab driver said. We make the stars. We build them, we give them the green light. The cabbie should have added something else. We tell them to raise all the hell they want, but we reserve the right to moralize over them.

Al dried himself and discovered a pair of silk pajamas and a robe at the foot of the bed. He picked up the jacket before he noticed the monogram on the pocket. J. F. He let it drop and got into bed. Almost immediately he fell into a deep, fettered sleep.

Virginia insisted on dancing. It was a dance of sinew and excitement, and with it she sang "Lullaby of Broadway," the song she had sung on his television show. When he caught her in his arms in a bear hug, she let out a slight cry and whimpered, "Daddy, you hurt me."

"You love me?" he demanded.

A vague fear shot through her, but it was fear mingled with bravado.

"Yes! I love you!"

"Tell me I'm the only guy, goddamnit!"

"The only! The only one! I'm crazy about—"

"Goddamnit, I need love! I gotta have love! God-damnit, you love me!"

CHAPTER FOUR

JOEY WOKE UP in panic.

His body was bathed in sweat and his hands trembled. Had he been screaming in his sleep? His throat was raw, as if he had. The room was in total darkness; the blinds were drawn and no light came through from the night outside. Hoarsely he called, "Honey?" and groped in the space beside him. No one was there.

"Honey?" he called again. He leaped up, terrified. He heard the ticking of his clock, and nothing more. He switched on the table light.

Alone. He was alone. And outraged and frightened at being alone.

He lifted the clock. Five-fifty. Hell, he'd turned over only a half hour ago! Why a nightmare? He hadn't overeaten. Damn Italian food usually gave him nightmares, but he'd been cutting down.

"Honey?" he called again.

Now he could not control his breathing. He opened his door and ran out into the hall. "Clyde?" he called. "Clyde, are you here?" He hurried until he came to Al's room. He pounded on the door and cried out, "Al! You in there? Al? It's me! Open up, Al, you hear?" God, God, what if Al were out? Al and Clyde and the chick? What if he were alone, alone, *alone* in the whole apartment! "Al! Al! Al!" he screamed.

"Joe?" The door sprang open and Al stood there, worried. He turned on the overhead light and his hand touched Joe. "Joe! What's the matter?"

For a while—he didn't know how long—Joey stood before his brother, struggling to organize himself, to control his breathing.

"Joe! You all right?"

"Whu you—"

"Come on. Sit down."

"Where you been?"

"Here, Joe. Come on, sit down. What happened?" He guided him to the edge of the small bed. The muscles in Joe's neck were taut, and his eyes, though no longer terrified, merely stared ahead.

"Wait, Joe. I'll get you a drink."

Al started for the door, but Joe sat forward and lifted his hands. "No! Don't go! Don't leave! Stay here!"

Al came back. "You have a nightmare, boy?"

"I— Yeah. Don't go."

"All right, fella."

"Chick. The chick, she isn't here. Isn't anywhere in the room."

"Joe, you're shaking. What is it, Joe?"

"I need a shot."

"There's some in the living room. Want to come with me?"

"A stiff one. Then I'll be O.K."

"You want to come with me?"

Joe looked up. "Whadda I wanna go with you for? Get me a drink, Al."

"You going to be all right, Joe?"

"I'll be all right."

"There's my robe. Put it on."

He sat for a moment on the bed, still feeling contortions in his legs and thighs. He leaned over and switched on another lamp to give the room more light. He was cold. He drew Al's robe up and wrapped it around him. His hand dug into the pocket and he brought out a crumpled cigarette. He inhaled once and coughed. Thank God for Al. Thank God somebody was home. He'd laid out his fear so plainly that anyone could see it, but Al was a bright kid. Al wouldn't laugh at him.

God, what was happening to him? He dreamed, sure, like anybody else. Bad dreams, dreams that made him feel wrung out and sick in the morning, but that happened to everybody, didn't it? Had he really screamed? Oh, baby, what an item for Walter's column! "What TV comic is keeping the neighbors up with his nightmare screams?" Oh, baby, how Broadway would love to get its teeth in that one!

Joe stared out at the night, blindly. Lory had been in the dream. Lory Kimball, flirting with him. He wanted her; nothing else mattered. She was handing him some kind of line with Shakespeare in it, or some broken-down poetry, but that didn't matter. His heart began pounding. This was Lory, the chick with class, the chick who had it all over the high-priced junk he wasted his time with. He started for her. He began to unbutton his shirt. But hell, he wasn't wearing a shirt. He had on the butcher costume for this week's opening sketch. He cursed the tight way the apron was tied around him, but he was going to get it off. He started unwinding the apron strings, but the more he unwound, the more string there was. Lory shot him a glance, impatient. But still the apron wouldn't come off, and when he looked down he saw yards of string. She shook her head. "I'm leaving," she said. "Got to make a show." He ordered her to wait, he'd be just a minute. She didn't like to be ordered. He pleaded with her. "One minute!" he begged. "One minute! Where you running?" He started for her. He came closer. She was laughing now. But not the friendly laugh. It was hard, tough, mean. The same laugh, the same standard brand that all the others with the dyed hair handed him. "Shut up!" he said. But she laughed louder. He couldn't control himself; he started to cry. He was swearing, begging, threatening. He came closer. He lowered his hands. Damnit, he'd make her stop laughing! If he had to strangle her, put his hands around her neck and choke her to death, he'd make her stop laughing at him. But then it happened. She wasn't Lory any more. She was Al. It was Lory's body, but the head was Al's.

He could still hear her laughing. But Al was laughing, too. Hard and tough and mean, too. The laughter got stronger, meaner. Joey tried to stop crying. "Shut up, you hear me?" But they laughed. The noise was louder than anything he'd ever heard. His ears hurt and his throat was closing up. He screamed at the top of his lungs then, "Shut—up!"

Al was beside him, pouring a stiff shot into a tall glass. Joe accepted it greedily and drank without stopping, until liquor ran down the sides of his mouth. He coughed and handed the glass back to Al.

"How is it, Joe?"

"O.K. Give me a cigarette, will ya?"

"You're holding one in your hand, Joe."

Joe moved to the half-opened window and stared out onto what could be seen of the courtyard. A few lights were on in apartments across the yard. The shades were drawn except in one room. His eyes followed that light and he could just see an old lady sitting by her window, rocking, reading, stroking a dog or a cat.

He heard Al's solemn voice. "Want to talk, Joe?"

Joe said slowly, "I don't know what's happening with me, Al." He pressed his forehead against the pane. It was cold.

"Was it a bad dream?"

Joe nodded.

"We all have them."

"I'm shot, kid. I feel like I'm outside my skin, lookin' around, sayin', 'Let me out of here. Damn cage is-boxin' me up.' " He could see now it was a cat on the old lady's lap. "What would an old dame be doin' up, six o'clock in the morning?"

"Old dame?" Al raised his head and saw her. "I don't know."

"Chickens don't even get up that early on the farm." He brought the cigarette up to his lips but it wouldn't draw. It had gone out. He flicked it out the window and listened for a while, as if he might be able to hear it fall to the concrete yard, seventeen floors below.

"Joe, what's eating you?"

He shrugged. "If I knew, we'd both know."

"Virginia was in here."

"Virginia?"

"Virginia, remember? The girl I brought home."

"When was she here?"

"Ten, fifteen minutes before you got here. She knocked on my door, woke me up. Said she was leaving."

Joe wheeled around and looked at him. "What the hell for?"

"Funny kid. She said she had to leave, she was afraid to stay here with you."

"Ten minutes ago?"

Al nodded. "About. Were you trying to strangle her, Joe?"

"Strang— Will somebody let me in on this?"

"I thought for a minute maybe she was the one with the imagination. She said she'd known you for a while but this was the first time you really got rough. She said you started groaning in your sleep, muttering something. She told you to take it easy and you did for a while, then you started talking. She says you put your hands around her neck."

"She's out of her head!"

"Is she, Joe?"

"God sakes, what am I, a loony? She's bats!"

"She tried to wake you up, but she couldn't."

"Awright, I sleep like the dead. She was the one dreamin'."

"So she cleared out. What's the trouble, Joe?"

"No trouble!" He paced the room. He took a cigarette from the bureau and lighted it.

"Let's have it, Joey. Something's on your mind. Don't hold it in. Gets bottled up that way."

"This room's creepin' inside me. Let's go in the kitchen, make same coffee or something. Come on."

No, the kid couldn't be that bats, Joey knew. He walked quickly from room to room, switching on lights as he went. Was he cracking, really cracking? The doc had told him nobody could keep this work schedule up, day after day, on three, four hours' sleep. The doc had given him some fifty-dollar words about going to see a psych, patching up whatever was kicking at him. Psych. He made more dough than a whole goddamn schoolful of psych doctors and he had more friends, more laughs, more on the ball than a schoolful of psych doctors. Who was trying to tell *him* he was going bats?

He went into the kitchen and switched on the light. He fumbled through an enormous stock of cans and jars in the cupboard and found some powdered coffee. He let some water splatter into a pot and heated it. He looked for a cigarette, found one, and lighted it. Then he saw he still had one, only half smoked, in his hand. He tossed both of them into the sink.

When Al appeared, Joey sank to a chair at the kitchen table. Good kid, Al. Didn't hit him over the ear with a pack of questions. Maybe Al was the boy to talk to, the whole story. Confession-good-for-the-soul stuff. Why not? What the devil had he told him to come to New York for, anyway? He didn't know, really. At the time it had seemed right, the only thing to do. Al had looked like the only guy to pour it on. And here was Al, good old Al, getting coffee ready, willing to listen.

"Let's hear about it, Joe."

"Maybe tomorrow. I don't feel like talkin'."

"The coffee's boiling. It'll take five minutes to drink it. Can't hurt to talk."

You wise-guy punk, Joey thought, you cultured-pearl punk. I must be skating on the doorknob, after all. Me, Joey French, and I'm scared of a two-bit punk like you. You don't have two bits in your pocket. Why'd I call you out to New York? What did I need you for? You were the one who got lost, you were the one who tried to get to the top and didn't make it. I made the name. Why should I feel like a kid in front of you? Who are you to—

Tears welled up inside him and, before he could control himself, he began to cry.

Al waited.

"Why the hell'm I bawlin'?"

Al spoke gently. "What's it all about, Joe?"

He tried desperately to stop, but his body quivered and the strength of control wasn't there. Al brought him a paper towel from the wall. He blew his nose and nodded. Then there was nothing to do but talk.

"I know five thousand people in this town by their first names. From bookies up to the president of the Chase National Bank. I'm shakin', though. I figured, let me get this high, let me thumb my nose at everyone who said I'd never make it, let me get where I wanted to get, an' there wouldn't be those damn shadows any more."

"Shadows?"

"Shadows. Every time I walk I feel like I got somep'm in back of me, somep'm startin' to climb on my neck, not lettin' me relax for a second." Bravely he brought his head up and looked at Al. He had uncorked his bottle of secrets and now he needed to talk. "I checked with a doctor the other day. I don't know what sent me there; I had a million things on the schedule. Yes, I know why I went. I tried to laugh it off, forget it. But I was scared. You ever been scared?"

"Yes."

"I'm married three times, Al. You remember Gloria; the others you never met. Never worked out, none of them. Always lookin' for the right girl, right woman. If I find the right one, I figured, I'm all set. Career's made an' all I need is the right woman, an' I don't have to get these crazy thoughts. I don't know what it is, I've always had it, but lately it's getting worse. Dames. I gotta go for them. The world can come to an end, I gotta have 'em. Like bein' on horse, a guy's not responsible, ya know? That isn't right. Awright, a yen, you get a yen for a chick, you wait.

You hold out an' you wait for the right time. But it's gettin' worse with me, Al. It's like another man's inside me, I can't get him out. Drives me bugs.

"Couple years ago, this year, it pops up, but not so bad. I'm in the middle of a rehearsal or in conference on the picture I'm shootin' next summer, and bang, seems like nothing else matters. But I hold tight, I wait. Then the other day, three days ago, that was—that was new."

"What happened three days ago?"

"I hit bottom. Who'm I gonna turn to an' tell such a thing? Three days ago I'm sittin' in Bucky Ahearne's office, workin' out next week's guest line-up. Virginia's sittin' across the room, not sayin' a word. An' I got my mind on work. Anyway, she drops her cigarette holder and she leans over to pick it up. All of a sudden, nothing else counts."

Al poured the boiling water, added coffee, and handed Joe a cup.

"Look, this kinda thing's O.K. for the kids, for the squares, for the small-timers. But I'm big league. Bucky knows me like a brother, but after all, I gotta act big league, don't I?"

"What happened?"

"I guess I went crazy, and when I came out of it I was sick. Bucky looked like he was ready to call the psycho ward." He waited again and, his voice trembling, he asked, "Ja ever hear such a thing, Al?"

"Is this doctor you went to see a psychiatrist?"

"No. He gave me the name of a guy. Expensive as hell, over on Park. Like lyin' on a couch and talkin' about bein' scared by a box of corn flakes when I was two years old is gonna straighten me out. I said the hell with it."

"Maybe a psychiatrist's the answer, Joe."

Joey shook his head. "No. Five times a week he wants me to go there. Where the hell'm I gonna find five free hours a week? You saw my schedule. No, I just need somebody to look after me,

like I said. Al, I'm afraid sometimes like the day'll come I'm doin'
a show on TV an'—"

"What's the psychiatrist's name?"

"Why?"

"I'm going to phone him at nine o'clock."

Joey's eyebrows arched as though he'd been betrayed. He
pushed the cup from him and stood up.

"I didn't call you here for that kind of help."

"How can I help you, then?"

Joey walked away. "Forget it. Go back to sleep. I'll be all
right."

Al followed him, frowning. He reached for the big man's
arm. "Joe, I'll give it to you straight. I knew you had your problems, but this is too big. You're killing yourself this way. This is
sickness, Joe. The worst sickness I've seen since I've been in town.
Go for that help, you understand? You've got to if—"

There was a telephone in the hall. Joey stopped and studied
it, as if he were seeing it for the first time. Al watched him, angry
yet helpless. A minute went by, then Joey picked up the receiver.
He dialed with only sullen interest.

"Who are you calling, Joe?"

"Never mind. Turn in."

"Who are you calling?"

Joey looked at him and said irritably, "Knock it off, will ya?"

"You phoning the psychiatrist?"

"Yeah. The psych."

Al leaned against the wall, his hands in the pockets of his
robe. He still watched his brother. Soon Joey's shoulders rose,
and again he was Joey French, the Million-Dollar Dynamo.

"Lou? Yeah, the Great Man. How are ya, doll baby? ... No,
nothin's up.... Whaddaya mean, six o'clock in the morning?
It's ha' past six, you loafer!" He chuckled and scratched his arm.
"Listen, Lou, why I called: Get Betty up an' bring her over.... No,
I'm not nuts, I'm lonesome. An' I'll tell you: Call up Bernie an'

Whatser-name with the Southern drawl.... So what, ha' past six? You and I got an appointment at ten, anyway, here, don't we? So we'll pass the time till the appointment gets under way.... O.K., speed it up, doll baby. Can't live without you bums.... Ha-ha. The same to you. Double.... Yeah, fast as you can make it."

CHAPTER FIVE

A N INSISTENT whirring sound from another room wakened Al a little before eleven. It was a DC-6 they'd tried vainly to teach him to fly when he'd found himself to be an officer and gentleman in the Air Force. He sat up and listened. No, it was a vacuum cleaner. He punched the pillow and thought wistfully of a rent-free forest where he could sleep the clock around. The strident laughs, the shrill yips he'd heard at seven and seven-thirty and seven-forty-five and later had wakened him, but only for a minute at a time. Finally he had drifted into a restless sleep.

He looked for the robe and recalled Joe had been wearing it. He opened a closet. He found six robes hanging there, each a different color and texture, and he wasn't surprised. Robes had always been a fetish with Joe, even in the thirty-dollar-a-month days. Al chose a bright foulard, got into it, and opened the door. The vacuum's dull roar stopped suddenly.

A maid looked up guiltily. "I bet I woke you."

Al smiled. "Glad you did. I would've slept all day."

"I'm sorry, anyhow," she said. "But there just isn't no other time to clean. The way they live around here, touch and go, I sort of have to follow their schedule, and they don't even *have* a schedule."

"Must be rough. What's your name?"

"Gladys. You're Mr. French's brother, aren't you?"

Al nodded. "Yes. Is he here, by the way?"

Gladys set the vacuum close to the corridor wall and pushed back wisps of gray hair. "He's got a run-through going on now in the living room. They're readin' for next week's show. If you want to shower and all, you can close the door and I'll make up your room."

Al started back. "No hurry, Gladys. I *would* like to get a suit pressed, though. Think that could be arranged?"

Gladys followed him into the room. "There's a cleaner on the ground floor. I can send a suit down and have it pressed in fifteen, twenty minutes. Want to send some others down, too?"

"All right, if you will."

"And coffee's ready, if you'd like some."

"Swell."

Al showered and shaved and came out of the bathroom to find a pressed suit hanging in the closet and a carafe of coffee on the night table. He sat on the bed's edge and poured a cup. This was living. This at-the-fingertips service was impressive and he was enjoying it, particularly because it was all earned by the cafeteria comic whom nobody had ever expected to make a buck. Of course, last night hadn't been pleasant. He would have to help Joey some way, any way he could. But first he would have to find himself before he could begin to find Joe.

Al dressed and felt relatively fresh as he stepped out of his room and into the hall. He could hear a chorus of voices now, and a piano in a ragtime bit. He saw Gladys, who nodded cheerfully.

"Breakfast's ready," she said, and pointed down the hall. "Keep going straight and you'll find the kitchen, if you don't mind eatin' there. They're makin' too big a racket in the living room to eat anywheres else but the kitchen."

"Kitchen's fine, Gladys."

"Rose is there gettin' it for you. If she sasses you, sass her back. She's that type; talks a lot."

He had to pass the living room. He tried to move by as unobtrusively as possible, but he was seen by nearly every one of the rehearsers. Joey, wearing a terry-cloth robe and carrying a glass of milk, was pacing nervously around the piano, running through some special material. A languidly beautiful girl was accompanying him at the piano and six of eight actors were sprawled on sofas and chairs, watching for cues. A few of them waved to Al and he smiled and nodded. Joey was putting life into the song, but his expression was tight and concentrated. He broke off suddenly and barked, "C'mon, honey, whaddaya say? *Two-four, two-four*! Don't fall asleep on me. Awright, try it again. From 'I'll put a lamp shade on my head at the party.' "

In the kitchen Rose nodded curtly and motioned for Al to sit at the table. He tried to strike up a conversation but Rose was stolidly silent.

He could hear the music stop again. Joe was shouting something, angry. "—that way Wednesday night, we'll *all* get pink slips! Start again! Two-*four*!"

Al looked up. "Rose, would you happen to know the name of Mr. French's doctor?"

"Doctor?"

"Uh, yes. I think I wrenched my arm yesterday and I want to have it looked at."

Rose shook her head. "I don't know."

"O.K. Thanks."

Then he heard a crisp voice, almost at his elbow. "Mr. French?" He looked up. It was one of the men he'd seen in the living room, young and tall and cheerful. Except for heavy glasses and thick black hair, this man bore a striking resemblance to Joe.

"Good morning," he said, and pumped Al's hand. "I'm Clyde Waverley, Joe's right arm."

"Oh, yes. How are you? I'm just finishing."

Waverley sat across from him, moving with much the same kinetic energy that was Joe's trade-mark. "No, no. Go right ahead. I just wanted to say hello. Joe asked me to tell you he's got a backbreaker today for a schedule and would you mind shifting a little on your own for a day or so?"

"Sure, I understand."

"He's in one of those hassels a day before the show; you know how it is. You're in the business yourself, aren't you? What is it again? You work for a record outfit or something, don't you?"

Al grinned. "I play records. Radio."

Waverley snapped his fingers. "That's right. He did tell me." Rose started to leave the room. Al thought he detected a mild sneer in her attitude toward Waverley. She went out. "I make out Joey's itinerary from morning to night. Maybe I can help you find your way around town for a day. Show tickets, the fights, a girl . ."

"Thanks, but I'll just get my city legs for a while. Oh, maybe you *can* help me. Joe's doctor ... "

Waverley looked up, toward the door. Joey was coming at them, quickly, a sheaf of papers in one hand, the glass of milk in the other. Waverley half rose.

Joey looked at Al as if Al were the only other man in the room.

"Are you still foolin' around with songs and music?"

Al smiled. "Fooling around's the best way to say it."

Joey went on, rejecting banter. "If it goes right, would you be willing to take over on the show? Music director?"

"Mu-"

"It'd be a month or so from now and it'd have to be O.K.'d by Bergman at the big desk. But if that goes through an' you can score a show, how about it?"

"Well,

"C'mon, c'mon. Yes? No?"

"Yes."

Joey clumped out of the kitchen.

Al sat up, a little dazed. He glanced at Waverley, who, having risen, was winking at him.

"Not bad, fella!"

Suddenly Joey's voice sounded again, a fierce bellow.

"*Clyde!* Get the hell *in* here! We don't have all *month!*"

Waverley was up before Joe's voice died away. The stridency in the call wakened Al. He touched Waverley's arm.

"Just one question before you go. Who's Joe's doctor?"

"Huh?"

"Wrench in my arm. Do you know his doctor's name?"

"Wait a moment. Han ... Hask ... That's right, Haskill. On Lex, I think." He darted out.

The kitchen clock read eleven-forty. Al drained his cup and got up, trying to recall the layout of as much of the apartment as he'd seen last night. He found the study without too much trouble, and closed the door behind him. It was a small room with a large, cluttered desk and book-lined walls. Al lifted the desk phone and pulled the monogrammed address book from beneath it. His finger riffled the pages until he found H. "Dr. A. H. Haskill." He picked up the receiver and dialed.

He gave the girl his name and waited, his foot tapping anxiously on the carpet. Idly his eyes roved over the address book. He read Don Haven's name and phone number five or six lines under Haskill's. What the hell's he got Haven's name here for? he wondered.

When he heard Dr. Haskill's voice he said, "I'm Alan French, Doctor; Joe's brother."

"Yes. Call me in, say, fifteen minutes, will you, please, Mr. French? I'll have time to talk then."

Al went back to his room and slung his topcoat over an arm. As he headed for the front door, Waverley stopped him and handed him an envelope.

"Joey asked me to give you this," he said, and hurried off.

While he waited for the elevator, Al opened the envelope. He counted one hundred dollars in ten-dollar bills.

Dr. Haskill apologized for having been so brusque, when Al phoned from a drugstore booth. "But I don't know what help I can give you or your brother, Mr. French. I made a suggestion. The rest is up to him."

"How serious is it, Doctor?"

"I'm a physician, Mr. French, and I won't diagnose anything that's not in my book. I told him about Dr. Kleiner and I suggested he see him. You say you haven't seen your brother for a long time?"

"Ten years. We talked for just a few minutes last night and none of it sounded good. I simply want to know this, sir: How serious is it?"

"Briefly, it amounts to this: He's losing control of his impulses, and that's serious enough. But no physician can really cure him, nor can any physician force him to see Dr. Kleiner. Let me say this, Mr. French, and then I've got to see my next patient: Do what you can to get him there. Or at least try to make him rest. Otherwise, he may crack up, and anything can happen."

"Then he knows what the situation is?"

"Completely. If he goes on without help or rest much longer, he's acting out the suicide urge."

"That sounds a little frightening, Doctor."

"It is."

"Thank you, Doctor."

Al sat in the booth and stared at the floor until he heard someone rapping on the glass. He got out and left the drugstore.

It doesn't make sense, Al thought, as he crossed Fifth. Sure, the pressure of work can be killing, but there must be a raft of people with pressures that tough. Joe's a clown! That kind of guy doesn't... They say this sort of thing doesn't pop up out of nowhere. They say it's got to be planted in childhood or it won't happen at all; something about misdirection when you're a kid. So why Joe? Joe was the happiest kid alive. Never cried, never got sore. Why is he headed for a million-an-hour psych now? We were poor, O.K., but hell, who wasn't poor? And who had modern, textbook parents who understood child psychology? So Pop wasn't the kindest man alive; so what? And Ma didn't live as long as she could have. Is that a reason? Is there a reason?

"Watch it, Mac!"

Al looked up, startled. He'd jostled someone. "Sorry," he said. He looked at the street sign. He was at 51st and Seventh. He blinked and shook his head. He'd walked all this distance without knowing it.

He found himself beside another phone booth, racing his finger down the Manhattan book. He called Dr. Kleiner.

As he waited he reached for a cigarette, and touched the envelope in his coat pocket. That would have to be straightened out, he thought. That would definitely have to be straightened out.

"—quite busy, Mr. French. And, besides, what could I do?"

"You're right, Doctor, but if I could make an appointment with you ... "

"I understand your concern, Mr. French. But there's nothing I can discuss with you until I've seen and talked with the patient. And Dr. Haskill informs me that isn't likely at the moment. Even then, I would require permission from my patient before I would discuss anything with relatives or friends."

"Dr. Kleiner, I'm simply trying to get a course of action so I'll know what to do."

"When he's ready to see me, send him in. That's all I can say, Mr. French. Will you excuse me now? I'm quite busy."

Al went to the Manhattan book once more, aware that he was grasping at straws now. He recalled having read in Variety that Joe was represented by the Bucklin Ahearne Agency. And Joe had mentioned Ahearne last night.

"Yeah, Joe's talked a lot about you," Ahearne rasped into the phone. "I've heard a lot about the kid brother. Joey told me I don't know how many times that you've got all the brains in the family."

"What about a lunch date, Mr. Ahearne?"

"Today's hell, I can tell you that right now. What about two, three days from now? You said yourself you just got to town. Let's say next Monday. How's that?"

Al paused a moment and then said quietly, "Let me know one thing. Joe told me a gruesome story about himself in your office. Was it true?"

There was a pause. Then Ahearne said, "Yeah."

"When can you meet me?"

"How's five-thirty, thereabouts?"

"All right."

"The Roosevelt. We'll have a drink."

"Five-thirty at the Roosevelt."

Al walked to Broadway and fought to keep from thinking about Joey until five-thirty at the Roosevelt. There were other developments now. Joe had mentioned the job as musical director. Al hadn't considered working for Joe, taking anything from Joe. On the Coast, he had received what he'd read as an SOS and he'd come because his brother had needed him. But maybe the job made sense, Al thought. He could handle it, he was sure. He knew Paul Graffe and Herb Graham, TV musical directors, and though he'd got drunk with them and liked them, he was positive he knew more about scoring a show than both of them together. And what he didn't know could be learned. What about the disc job on KJK? That was no real problem. A long-distance call to Bill Kunstler ... Why not? Al frowned and walked a little faster. If I can shape myself here and do something for Joe at the same time—why the hell not?

He went on down Broadway, feeling stronger and equal to the city.

His eyes rose to a sign high above a tall building: "CLOUD NUMBER SEVEN, the hilarious comedy by Drew Branding, starring Lory Kimball. Strauss Theatre." On an impulse, noticing it was only a quarter past twelve, Al walked in the direction of the Strauss. There was a single seat left for the afternoon's performance, and Al bought it.

He had seen pictures of Lory Kimball in the Sunday Times drama section once or twice, but now he hadn't the faintest recollection of what she looked like. He studied the half-dozen photographs in the theatre lobby. She'd never do in Hollywood, he decided; her eyes were too far apart and her nose was a little too pointed to be commercial. But, he thought, she's a mighty handsome girl.

As he watched the play that afternoon he was pleased that she was as good as he'd hoped she would be. He tried to picture her as Joe's girl, as being anything related to Joe, and the image seemed contrived. There was an inner peacefulness in her performance, and she looked like a woman who would be discriminate in her choice of men. His eyes kept roving to his wrist watch, and his mind to thoughts of Joe and Ahearne. Restless, he left the theatre during the second intermission.

Bucklin Ahearne was a beefy, red-faced man with an infectious laugh. He was in his fifties, with a meat-grinder voice.

"How's this table, Al? Don't mind if I call you Al?" He smiled warmly, and ordered for both of them. He settled his bulk into the chair. "I got a ticker like a bum tire. Liable to give like that." He snapped his stubby fingers. "You'd think liquor would be posion for me. But my doctor—sometimes I call him Caligari—says alchohol can't hurt me. Go try to figure it."

Al said something perfunctory. Ahearne recognized his impatience and nodded. "We're not here about the old angina, are we? We're here about Joey."

"I'm up a tree, Mr. Ahearne."

"Bucky."

"His doctor can't treat him physically. The analyst can't treat him unless he shows up. Joe's on stage for a twenty-four-hour day. What the hell good did I do coming to New York?"

"How important to you is it for Joey to stay on the "ball?

"Oh, come on!"

"Mmm. All right, I'll tell you where Joey stands as of today. He knows this as well as I do, so I'm not gossiping behind his back. The second wrong step he takes will be on my shoulders, nobody else's, and the sponsor and the network will be after my neck. That's why he's got to be careful not to take the first wrong step. It isn't only Joey, although I love him. It's that an army of people depend on his well-being for their livelihood. Clear? If he took a month off and went to Florida, maybe that would snap him out of it. I don't know. I'm no doctor. But I've sent up the smoke signal for him, Al, and he knows he's in trouble. How much did he tell you?"

"Very little. Only the business in your office the other day."

"Yeah. There's more. So far his shows are still going smoothly, but we've had four girls quit because he got a yen for them in rehearsals and let 'em know it. Nothing to really make you lift the eyebrows, but enough to make you see something's pressing him hard. The hell of it is that he knows what's happening. Just the crazy behavior that comes and goes. He worries about it and then the next minute he convinces you nothing'll happen again, so we've been coasting along for a while, keeping our fingers crossed. But he isn't my only account, Al. He makes money for us, but we can't act as his armed guards."

"When did it begin? When did you first notice it?"

Ahearne shrugged. "It's not something that hits you in the teeth. Joey's always lived hard and rushed, you must know that. Maybe it's that screwball crowd he hangs out with. Listen, Al, let's put it on the line. I'm a friend, but I've got to protect Bucky Ahearne. If Joey takes that wrong step, he'll be replaced on Channel Three by juggling seals. It's as simple as that."

Al heard Ginny Hutch's voice as he entered Joe's apartment.

"Awright, don't get sore, Clyde. I'm just asking where he's at. What's there to get sore about?"

He went into the living room and saw Clyde Waverley at the sofa, sorting papers on a hassock that served as a makeshift desk. Virginia was moving about tentatively, trying to get Clyde's attention, trying to cajole him into a conversation. She wasn't nearly so self-possessed as Al had seen her last night. She wore a low-cut blue dress, and her hair was swept up adultly. She was obviously anxious but there was something in Clyde's attitude that restrained her from unleashing what emotion she felt.

"Clyde, I'm asking you a question."

Waverly's head shot up in annoyance. "I told you a dozen times: He's got a conference! Now will you clear out, Ginny, and let me work? I'm not Joey's housemother."

They both saw him at the same time. Clyde seemed embarrassed. Ginny stretched out a hand, smiling hopefully, as if Al had all the answers.

"Hey, man!" she cried. "Dig you the most!"

"Hello, Ginny," Al said, and exchanged nods with Clyde. He freed himself from her embrace and went to the bar. "I break anything up?"

Clyde returned to the papers. "No, Ginny was just leaving."

Ginny followed Al and watched him pour a straight Scotch. "Al, do you happen to know where Joey's at?" she asked with a desperate lilt.

He shook his head and heard Clyde say, "I've told you, Ginny. He left word that he'll contact you tomorrow at the phone service. He's meeting Bucky Ahearne. How about shoving off?"

She still faced Al. "Looks like I'm not wanted, doesn't it, Professor?"

Al swallowed and answered softly, "Seems so, Ginny."

"Did I tell you a fella told me I might get on a cover of Life magazine?"

"Wonderful."

Ginny paused, then looked from Al to Clyde and back to Al again. The silence cut into the walls of the room. Even Clyde's rustle of papers ceased.

"So I get kicked out on my fanny, huh?"

More silence.

Al could see her feet move slightly. "You know, I don't have to take this," she said without open hostility. "I wasn't born on a farm in Kokomo. I know when somebody's tryin' to give me the rush act."

Clyde looked up. "When does this curtain fall?"

"Where's he at, Clyde? I'm asking you for the last time. You be civil to me or I'll make more trouble for you than you ever—"

He rose from the couch. His mouth tightened in a quiet viciousness that sent the threat from Ginny's voice.

"I just wanna know about Margot Connell, that's all."

"Out," he said.

"He's going to that party, then, isn't he? To meet Lory Kimball. That's what all that talk about conference, conference is. Well, where do *I* come in?"

Clyde was firmly moving her to the door. He spoke in little more than a whisper, but Al could hear. "I don't repeat myself. You wait till you hear from Joe, and in the meantime keep out of my hair and everyone else's."

"Who you talkin' to?"

"You, brat. Now go peddle it somewhere else."

"You dirty—"

The door closed.

"Charming child, isn't she?" Clyde remarked, returning. "I didn't take a B.A. at Carnegie Tech to play wet nurse to juvenile delinquents."

Al reached for the Scotch bottle again. "Where *is* Joe, anyway?"

"He left a message for you. You're to meet him at Margot Connell's tonight around eleven. She does a column in the Press-Dispatch."

"We've met."

"She's having a party. I'll find the address for you." Clyde began to gather up his papers. "Joey's out for dinner tonight. He's sorry about missing you."

"How long have you been with Joe, Clyde?"

"Me? Year, a little longer."

"How's his health?"

Clyde laughed. "Health? He's a dynamo, that Joey. Greatest guy in the world."

Al nodded.

"Will you excuse me now?" Waverley said. "I've got to run. Oh, if you haven't eaten yet, Rose's still here. I can tell her to get you some dinner."

"Great, Clyde. Thanks."

Al faced the window until the door opened and closed. He didn't know how long it was before he heard the telephone ring. He waited, feeling out of place for the hundredth time today. He looked around at the wide expanse of vacant room. There was a phone extension near him and its insistent ringing made the only dent in the soundless and shadowy apartment. He lifted the receiver.

"Joey, honey? This is Jean." It was a liquid, caressing voice.

"Jean?"

"*Jean,* you fathead! Long time no hear, honey!"

"This ... this ... this isn't Joey."

"Oh. Well, then, who is it?"

"Joe's brother."

"Al? Oh, I've heard *reams* about you! Your name's All You sound cute."

"Joe isn't here now. Can I—"

"He ever talk much about me, Al? I'm trying to have that corn ball buy me some dinner tonight, but how about you? Seeing as how it's all in the family, Joey wouldn't mind...."

CHAPTER SIX

ARGOT CONNELL'S large apartment was in pleasantly poor taste. Al looked around at the spacious room crowded with people. He recognized a few celebrities, none of whom he knew personally, and he was attracted to the raft of guests, who all looked so prosperous and freshly bathed and perfectly groomed. He saw neither Margot nor Osborne Colter.

He took a drink from a passing tray and went back to trying to identify people. It was quite a party. He hadn't seen anything like it since those brawls in Hollywood, in rooms where original Rouaults were scattered in rather than placed with scrupulous taste. The expensive paintings and first editions were in evidence here, too, but, like the Hollywood rooms he remembered, they gave the effect of their owners' wealth, and nothing more.

It was twenty of twelve, he noticed a few minutes later when he reached for his second drink. Margot Connell appeared from the welter of people and came toward him, calling, "Al! Hi!" Al finished the drink quickly, wishing suddenly he were completely sozzled.

"Al!" Margot said and took his arm. "How long've you been here?"

He smiled. "Just two drinks' worth, Margot."

Margot kissed him lightly and guided him in the direction of a cluster of people near the piano. She was wearing a gown—everyone except himself was in evening clothes, he realized now—and the gown, well cut and simple, made her seem a lot less severe than the Margot of the train.

"Everyone!" she announced, breaking into the frenzied conversations of a dozen people. "I want you all to meet Alan

French!" She offered his name, he thought, as if she were presenting someone of at least cabinet rank. But, except for a few polite hellos, no one was impressed. It was only when Margot continued with "Joey French's kid brother!" that some of them came to life. Al grinned and played along.

He accepted another drink and got into innocuous conversations, mostly with a blonde singer he remembered having met on the Coast. And then, goaded by his fifth drink—or was it sixth?—he found himself sitting at the piano, showing off with "Ain't Misbehavin' " and Gershwin's concerto.

Joey made a swaggering entrance at midnight—on the dot, Al noted—and fully half of the guests moved to him. He entered with Don Haven and a man Al had never seen before. He was calling, "Hello, Packy! Hey there, Charlotte! Hiya, Mitch!" and people responded almost in flurries. Al sat at the piano, trying to decide whether to rise or to wait for the Great One to come to him. Don Haven, accompanying Joe, disturbed Al. What are they doing together? he wondered.

"If I were you, heaven forbid," Al heard someone say, and looked up to find Osborne Colter leaning on the piano, "I'd sit still and let him pursue. I wouldn't be the one to burn incense."

Al frowned. Colter, dressed immaculately in an oldfashioned tuxedo, saw nothing, but obviously he knew what was going on in Al's mind. "You wouldn't, eh?" Al said.

Joey must have said something funny, for a chorus of laughter went up and Joey beamed at his audience.

"No," Colter replied. "I would tell myself, 'I'm tired of playing the constant youth, crouching in the shadow of fame. I'm going to be independent as the dickens.'"

"You're a little too esoteric, Mr. Colter," Al said.

Colter smiled, and managed to look bored. "Perhaps I am. Do as you will. It's a bit early in the evening to be swapping subtleties, anyway."

Joey waved an unlit cigar and invaded the room, flanked by Don Haven, who was hurriedly producing a lighter. "—so alla time he's tellin' me about Picasso," Joey was declaiming, his eyes roving around the room, as if he were a club manager counting the house, "and I'm noddin', actin' like I know what he's talkin' about, about this Picasso. So it's only when I says to him that the new models are better that he finds out I thought he was talkin' about Pierce Arrows!"

Satisfied with the affectionate response, Joey roared, "Hey, there's Al!" and came cross the room. He was dressed impeccably in evening clothes and he looked very much alive. Al rose slowly.

"Say, does everyone know we're father and son?" Joey asked, and looked around, making sure he was the center of attraction. He clapped his palm against the back of Al's neck and kissed his forehead. "Ladies an' gentlemen," he announced. "Al was the guy who told me all about the birds an' bees. He made it sound so good that I gave up women an' now I'm goin' out with birds and bees!" He laughed with the others and then tempered it for a moment as he saw Osborne Colter. "Hello, Poppy. How goes it?"

Colter nodded curtly. "Good evening," he said, and moved away. Margot heard the exchange and frowned fleetingly, but extended her hands to Joey.

"Joey," she said, "you've been holding out on us! None of us knew Al played so well."

Joey dropped to the bench beside Al, pushing Al a few inches away. He proceeded to play "God Bless America" with four-finger stiffness and answered Margot along with a large and interested audience. "Wadda you think? I want anybody to know somebody else got some talent in my family? Look, you mize well hear it now: Ol' Al's gonna take over the score of the show in a couple weeks. How's that for action?"

Al closed his eyes and listened without pleasure to the congratulations and applause. He fought a successful battle with rising anger, and when he opened his eyes again, Joe had risen and taken Margot's arm. Al heard him ask quietly, "Where's Lory, Marg? She was s'posed to be on deck tonight."

Margot patted his cheek. "Relax, Romeo. She wants to make an entrance, too, you know."

He was guided to the center of the room by Margot and some others, leaving Al alone once more. Al drained his glass and noticed Don Haven staring petulantly at him from the window. Al crossed to him.

"Hello, Haven," he said, and lifted a cigarette from a table. "Got a light?"

Haven produced a lighter and flicked it. He, too, wore evening clothes, but they seemed subdued beneath his yellow hair. He continued to stare at Al.

"What's wrong, Haven?"

"Sorry, Alan. I know staring is bad manners."

"Go on staring if you like. But I saw your face when Joe made his announcement."

Haven sank to the window seat and Al joined him. "Tsk." Haven grinned. "Am I as transparent as all that?"

"As I remember, you're a composer," Al said, looking intently at his cigarette.

Haven nodded.

"And you were waiting for the job. Right?"

"We'd—talked about it, yes."

"And this is the first you heard about me, hm?"

"It doesn't really matter."

"Doesn't it?" Al asked.

Haven shrugged, rose with a dancer's balance, and moved away. He turned his attention to Joey, who by now had taken complete charge of the evening. Al watched, too. Joey French, on stage, was doing the Moscow Art Threatre bit, a standard with him for years. It consisted of Joe's playing eight characters, changing his voice, inflections, and posture with each change of character. He acted out an intricate plot—all in Russian double talk—and his sharp sense of timing made it an effective piece of comedy. Only Don Haven was grave. His smile froze on his lips and his thoughts seemed far away.

Joey quieted appreciably in the next half hour, which produced no Lory Kimball. He sipped at his ginger ale and nervously fingered his jacket lapel. He would come alive for a moment when someone approached him and he would talk with animation. But his eyes gradually focused on the door and his volcanic energy appeared to be leaving him.

When she did arrive, Al was talking with a Negro doctor about modern composers. But their conversation dwindled mutually when Lory appeared. Margot and Joey were the first to reach her. Joey came back to life.

She was apologizing for being late, and Al could hear her apologizing too for not having dressed formally. She wore soft, pale tweeds that had been cut with mastery, and she was hatless, her ash-blonde hair shoulder length. She had a good face and figure, Al thought, and although she was chattering easily, she seemed as disinterested in being here as he was.

Al excused himself from the doctor and moved toward her. She was being polite to Joey, who was struggling to be fully accepted, but there was no real rapport, and this seemed entirely right. She didn't belong here, he thought; not with the Joey wing of the party, at any rate.

"You took your own sweet time," Joey was saying, a little unsure of himself. "I was all ready to send a posse out after you." He reached for her arm but she slipped away and smiled. Joey grinned, too, but it didn't reach his eyes.

She guided Margot to the buffet table, past Al, and Al heard her say, "Margot, I'm famished. Do you suppose I may have some of this delectable food?" Al glanced at Joey. He stood erect and a little stunned, unable to hide the disappointment from his face. His eyes followed Lory wistfully. Then, as if discovering he had exposed himself, he turned, chuckled, and was enveloped by a sea of attentive people.

Al continued to listen as Lory talked on. "We had a late curtain tonight and then some of the make-up got into my eye and it took days to get it out. Margot, don't hover like a mother hen. Let me eat and take care of myself and you go and greet everybody, yes?"

And then Margot was tugging at Al's arm. "Al, come here. I want you to meet Miss Kimball. This is Alan French, Lory."

Lory turned and her smile was casual. "Hello, Alan."

"Hello."

Margot said, "Al is Joey's kid brother."

"Isn't that fascinating," Lory said. "Help me pick out the imported from the domestic cheese, will you, Alan?"

"Well, I'll leave you two alone." Margot turned and looked at her party with an expert's eye.

They eyed one another furtively. Al raised two plates and offered one to her. "I didn't notice the buffet till now. You light up hidden corners, Lory."

She was calmer now as she shed the actress-at-a-party pose. "You enjoy being called the kid brother, don't you?" she asked dryly.

"Mm." He nodded. "It's something to live for. This cheese all right?"

"Fine."

They moved away and searched for a place to sit. Al didn't have to look up to know that Joe was watching their every step. They waited patiently, numbing themselves against the frantic noise around them, until they saw someone get up from a couch. Al pointed the way with his chin and Lory preceded him. Al followed, wondering what their two minutes together were meaning to her. Did she simply want to escape Joe? Was she merely being polite to Al? Or did she sense that they both shared the desire to get out of here?

"We made it!" she exclaimed, and sat aside to give him room.

"For a while it looked hopeless. Incidentally, whose guest are you tonight? Margot's? Colter's?"

"Margot's, I think. I agree to go to these things days and sometimes weeks ahead of time and then when I look at the schedule book again I grit my teeth. Or maybe I shouldn't say that. Is Margot your friend or aunt or something?"

He shook his head. "No, I'm in pretty much the same boat, except that my schedule book isn't quite so filled. You know what I'd like, Lory?"

"What?"

"I'd like us to hide these plates and go around the corner for a hamburger."

"Do you think we could?"

"Why not? I'm game."

She laughed softly. "I *would* love a hamburger, but everyone would get all hot and sensitive about it. I've got to pretend I'm having a wonderful time. But tell me about you, Alan. Are you married?"

"My wife is dead."

"Mmm. My husband's dead, too. What're you doing here? You're not happy playing Joey's kid brother."

"I got in from California just last night. I may work for Joe."

They saw Joey approaching them and they both looked up. "What about Joe?" he asked. "I hear my name taken in vain?"

"Joey!" Lory greeted. "Margot was telling me you were performing before and she said you were devastating. Why couldn't you have waited for me?"

He arched an eyebrow; Al didn't trust his friendliness. "Wait? Since when did you get interested in what I do?"

Her voice was cool. "Joey, you sweet lug, you know I'm enthralled by anything you do."

Al grinned irritably. He noticed Joe's silent order for him to get up and give the big boy a seat. But Al picked at his food, damned if he'd move.

"Well, well, well," Joey said and sat down on his heels. "If I'd of known that, I certainly would of waited an'—"

"—ey *French!*" They heard suddenly.

It was a shrill voice, coming from the front landing. Heads turned to the girl struggling past the butler and a cluster of guests. She was directing angry attention to Joey.

It was Ginny Hutch.

As she advanced, her shoulders moved curiously, as if she might be on marijuana. She was wearing the same orange coat, Al noticed, that she'd worn last night. Ineffable fury shone from her eyes. Al glanced at Joe, who rose slowly. His face was white.

"—not gonna make a jerk outta me, the baster'!" Her voice was husky and her fingers twitched nervously. Joey was on his feet, visibly embarrassed. People stopped talking and drinking to watch this new tableau. Margot was calling her back. Osborne Colter leaned against a table, a wan smile on his lips. One of his hands rested on his cane, the other in his pocket. His ankles were crossed.

"Two-timin' *me,* huh?"

Margot grabbed her arm and insisted, "Young lady, you get right—"

Ginny wheeled and slapped Margot hard across her eye. She turned back abruptly as Margot cried out, and faced Joey. His mouth hung open. Lory seemed fascinated.

"Big conference tonight, huh?" Ginny rasped, coming still closer, oblivious of all the others. "You hadda meet with some guys, huh, and talk about the show, huh? I asked you was you gonna come here tonight and you says no, you were busy tonight!"

Joe's embarrassment dissolved into an anger of his own. He took Ginny's hand with a savage movement.

"Easy, now," he whispered hoarsely.

She yanked her hand away, lost her balance, and bumped into someone behind her. "Don't you easy *me,* you two-timin' baster', you! What's a matter, I'm not good enough to come to these fancy parties with you, Mr. Big Shot? Huh?"

"Go on home," he snapped, barely holding back his rage.

"Don' *choo* tell *me* to go home! Don' *choo* order *me*, mister! I don' take orders from no two-timers nor nobody!"

"That's enough, now!" Joey cursed through his teeth and looked in helpless apology to all the people watching. He got her arm. "Get out and stay out!"

"Who you pushin' aroun'?" she shouted, and slapped at his head.

Joey pushed her away and tried to catch her as she lost her balance, but she fell to the floor, weeping wildly. "Don' choo—"

Mumbling, "I'm sorry, Margot," Joey bent over her. Her skirt had flown back and it seemed of vital importance for Joey to cover her legs.

Ginny rose by herself, eyes glittering, and pointed to Lory, who hadn't moved. "It's *her!* That's the one tryin' to get you now, isn't it? I'll kill 'er, tha's what I'll do! I'm good enough for you to take to Nora's an' the kids', but I'm not good enough to bring to these here fancy places, huh? That what choo tryin' a tell me?"

Al had never seen Joey so furious. He made his fingers into a fist and shot the fist down with resounding force into her jaw.

Somebody, not Ginny, screamed. Ginny herself shuddered, but neither spoke nor sobbed. She seemed numbed with fright by his angry strength. He paused just a moment, searching for breath, then took her by her coat sleeve. Roughly he pushed her forward until they were at the front door. He appeared now to be unconscious of anyone or anything but his overwhelming hatred for this girl. He opened the door and propelled her through it, his hand rough on the small of her back. He said something, but it was jumbled and incoherent.

He slammed the door and stood there for a few seconds, afraid to turn and face his audience. Of them all, only Osborne

Colter had continued to stand in precisely the same place, leaning against the table. He still smiled, a smile of pure malice.

Most of the guests strove to return to their light talk, although
each pair of eyes was on Joey French. When he did turn, he went
immediately in the direction of the bar. His face was still white
and he looked old. He pointed to a bottle of Scotch. The bartender poured a drink for him.

Lory lifted the plate of food on her lap and gave it to Al. She
looked at him and said, "I'm feeling just a little sick, Alan. Would
you take me out of here?"

CHAPTER SEVEN

SHE GAVE THE DRIVER a Houston Street address. Al lit a cigarette and gave it to her. He noticed that the taxi was making good time. The funny part of all these strange doings, Al thought, is that Joe's probably worked everything out by now and he's the life of the party again.

"I'm better now," she said suddenly, looking at him and smiling. They had been riding for twenty minutes or so. "I shouldn't've dragged you away."

"Do I looked dragged?"

"It's just that I'm an awful coward, Alan, when there's any sort of violence. You can drop me off any time you like."

"We talked about a hamburger, Lory. Remember?"

A dappled shadow fell across her as the cab stopped for a red light. Al looked at her now, and remembered her performance as the quick-witted lady of easy virtue in this afternoon's play. He was conscious of the fact that she'd been involved, or was now involved, in some way with Joe. But as the taxi started again, she had no relation with anything that had gone before. She was the tall, slim, and handsome girl he was seeing home.

"How long has your wife been dead, Alan?" she asked.

"Just a year," he said.

"Sudden?"

He nodded. "Hit by a car. Your husband in the war?"

Lory nodded. There was a long and perceptible pause, broken only when she indicated a squatty apartment house next to a delicatessen. Glumness left her and she became almost animated.

"That's the palace. Do you really want a hamburger? Come on up and help peel the onions."

It seemed unnecessary to ask why a girl who made quite a lot of money should live alone in two simple, nearly drab rooms in the Village. It was a third-floor walk-up that looked out onto a grim courtyard. None of the furniture matched. Nothing was really run down, Al decided; there was just a marked contrast to Joe's and Margot's sumptuousness.

Lory opened a closet door and brought out a robe. "Help yourself to the icebox, Alan," she said, and went into the bedroom. She kept the door open, but stood out of Alan's sight as she changed. "I seem to remember some hamburger somewhere. Maybe I was seeing things."

Al slowly paced around the apartment, looking at the shelves of books, the record player with stacks of good albums, the Degas prints. He noticed, between a Dubigny and a Greco, a framed cartoon of Mickey Mouse. He asked about it.

"Actually, I stole the idea from Nazimova," she called from the bedroom. "Nazimova owned a picture of Mickey Mouse, too, to teach her humility. She'd say, 'I can be called the greatest actress in the world and I can be idolized by every critic and audience of every country. I can be given the finest roles in the finest plays and I can give the finest performance. But ne-vair will my name ev-air be as well known as Meecky Mouze's.' "

She came to him then and he turned to look at her. Her robe was a quilted satin affair that hid the curves of her body but somehow accentuated the color in her cheeks. Al's stare held her and something in her eyes held him. He extended his arms and she came into them.

"You're mighty nice, Lory."

It was an eager, uncomplicated kiss. Al held her just a moment longer than seemed necessary; the instant he released her she crossed to the refrigerator and began to investigate.

"No hamburger," she confessed.

Al sat in the farthest chair. "I might have guessed."

"Cheese? Ham? Peanut butter?" she suggested. She set the food atop the closed phonograph and reached for some bottles in the closet. "What do you like, Alan? Bourbon, rye..."

"How about some milk?"

Lory looked up and grinned. "A hard-drinking man after my own heart." She poured two glasses of milk, fixed sandwiches, and sat across from him.

"There!" she declared. "Even my mother, who's an ironclad Baptist, couldn't find anything wrong with this."

They talked about harmless things as long as they could. Then Al brought it out in the open.

"Is Joey French sitting over there on the couch, Lory?"

She raised her eyes to his. "Not unless you invited him."

"I don't want to hurt the guy. Lory."

"I'm still my own woman, Alan. Mr. Lyons, Mr. Winchell, and Mr. Wilson seem to have us ready to get married, but it isn't true. I don't want anything from Joey. He's your brother and they say a lot of nice things about him, but I'm afraid I don't like him very much."

"Who do you like, Lory? Me, maybe, in time?"

"I like you already, Alan. But I've been in love before and it isn't much fun. I get ugly and brutal sometimes, so I develop claws to defend myself with. Does that make me sound crazy?"

"Just kind of."

"It would be easy to love you, but I'm not sure I want to."

"Shall I go, Lory?"

She nodded. "You do understand, Alan? I'm not ready to get involved with anyone yet."

Al rose and went to her. "Fair enough. But I want another kiss to make me uncomfortable after I leave."

Lory extended her hands. "Try and stop me."

Herb, the chauffeur, pressed the palm of his hand on the horn and cursed the driver ahead, who wouldn't give him room enough to pass. Joey called from the back seat, "Not so loud, Herb. It's after one."

He slouched and looked vacantly through the car window. He coughed and sat up again, noisily clearing his throat. "Gotta cut out so many cigarettes."

Don Haven, sitting next to him, lowered the window an inch. "My cigarette bothering you, Joey?"

Joey shook his head and refused to look at Don. He crossed his legs and uncrossed them. He took a cigarette from his case and lit it before he remembered his pledge.

Don's voice seemed far away. "Want to talk, Joey?"

"Whadda I wanna talk for?" he snarled, and glanced at Don for an instant. He knew he was in one of those godawful moods where he didn't know what the hell he wanted; a drink, a session with Nora's bop, a chick, lots of company.... He thought about Al and Lory and then about the Hutch kid, the kid who'd embarrassed him more than he'd ever been embarrassed in his life. Al wasn't to blame for anything. Al pulled the right rabbit out of the hat by getting Lory away; he should've done it sooner. It was that crazy kid who made him sore, so sore that he could punch his fist through this window right now. Well, he'd learned his lesson. From now on, no more kicking around with teen-age tramps like that. None of it's worth the grief. Al said that. Al was the only one who made sense in this whole crazy town. Keep away from kids.

"Joey?"

His head whipped up. "What? Whaddaya Joey, Joey, Joeyin' about?"

Don was insulted and leaned against his side of the automobile. "I'm sorry. I was just trying to help."

"I don't figure you, Haven. Whaddya get out of helpin' me? What's the ante for you, one way or the other?"

Don sat forward and pouted. "Maybe I'd do better to get off at the corner and go home."

"Awright, you know me. I don't mean anything I say."

"I consider you my friend, Joey. A friend likes to help another friend."

Joey nodded gloomily and stared at the floor of the car.

"I can understand your frustration perfectly," Don soothed. "No one likes that kind of notoriety, particularly from that type of person. You mark my words, Joey, she'll try to cause you trouble."

Joey chuckled harshly. "Cause trouble, uh? She didn't cause me enough already. Let 'er. Let 'em all yell. I don't bend down to the sponsor, I won't bend down to her."

"I know, I know. I just wanted to warn you. I'll do everything I can to help you, Joey, but she'll go on making trouble."

Joey's eyes narrowed. "You tell me something, will ya?"

"If I'm able."

"Can that stuff about friendship. Whaddaya want from me? Takin' over the show's score's just about sewed up now. Whadda you givin' me about you're my friend and all that?"

"You're wrought up, Joey."

"Come on, don't give me your vocabulary. You butterin' me up because you think I'll still give you the job?"

Don frowned and bit his lip. He stamped his cigarette into the ash tray. "We're getting close to your house. Let's go into this some other time."

Joey shrugged and the car pulled up to the front door.

"Want to put the firearms away, Joey, and ask me up for a drink?"

Joey's mind raced. Al might be in, might not. There was no telling about Clyde, and it would be hell being alone this early. He gazed at Herb, who had eyes and ears in the back of his head.

He'll have a ball, Joey thought, if he sees me takin' a queer up to the place.

"Hmm, Joey?"

"Uh ... lemme turn in, Don. Herb'll drop you off. I'm bushed tonight, wanna go to sleep. O.K.?"

"Certainly. I understand. I'll phone you."

"Yeah. Swell. G'night. Take him home, Herb."

You bucketbrain, Joey thought, as he swaggered into the plush lobby; you almost had one of those queens up to your pad. What's the idea nobody lets you rest? Who you punching for? Who gets your dough when you cash in? God, lemme rest, lemme lay down and take off my shoes and rest. What'm I tryin' to prove?

The elevator man set his paper down and hurried to his station. "H'lo, Mr. French. In early tonight, uh?"

Joey laughed and touched the man's shoulder affectionately. "Gettin' domesticated in my old age, Ernie. Say, how's the missus?"

Ernie shrugged. "Still with the arthritis."

"I told ya, ya stubborn old character. I'll give ya a thousand, you take her down to Warm Springs like I said."

"I know. That's awful nice, Mr. French, but it's the way I told you: She wouldn't leave Prospect Avenue for all the rice in China. I couldn't pick up and go, anyway. It just wouldn't work."

"Uh. Well, remember what I said. The minute you're set to leave, you let me know."

"Mighty nice, Mr. French."

The door purred open and Joey stepped into the private vestibule. "Night, Ernie."

"Good night, Mr. French." And he was alone.

He pressed the buzzer and hoped for someone, anyone. What'd I do wrong? he wondered, refusing to take out his key to let himself in; what'd I do to her to make her give me the ice-cube smile? It wasn't just the Hutch kid; I was talkin' to her before that, wasn't I? Wasn't I? She was sittin' with Al and I went over to her. Whatta I have to do to make her go for me? If I had her I wouldn't need another thing in the world! I told her I went for her, didn't I? Maybe I should've said something about getting married. Yeah, that might've made her look up and take notice. Me, I always got something to say, but when it counts I'm like deaf, dumb an' blind.

The door opened quickly, startling Joey. Clyde Waverley peered out, closed the door again, unhinged the latch, and admitted him. "Early for you, isn't it, Joey?"

"All right with you?"

"Sure, sure," Clyde answered, and took his coat. "I was just saying."

"Well, don't say. Fill the tub up."

"You turning in?"

Joey wheeled and barked, "What's this? Third degree? Whadda you care what I do? I told ya to fill up the tub. You wanna ask questions?"

Clyde was silent for a moment. Then: "O.K., Joey."

"Calls? Messages?" Joey started for the study and removed his tie. He took off his jacket and tuxedo shirt as he walked. Clyde followed him, picking them up.

"Jean Bixby phoned a few times, said you were supposed to contact her. Nothing else important. Oh, Ginny Hutch was here."

Joey turned. "Who told her about Margot Connell's party?"

"Don't tell me she showed up there!"

"I ast a question! How'd she find out where I was?"

"Honest to God, Joey, I don't know. She came here with all the information. I denied it all. I don't know where she learned it."

"What time was she here?"

"About seven. Your brother was here, too."

"He here now?"

"No, not yet. I was planning to leave when I finished the letters."

Joey entered the study. "Stick around till he shows up. Bring me a ginger ale."

Alone, he switched on the overhead light. An ache pounded in his head and he was tempted to get an aspirin. But he was distrustful of any pill and he vowed to forget the headache. He sat at the desk and stared at the clock. He reached for the address book. Call Jean, he thought, tell 'er to run over for an hour. What can it hurt? She at least knows the score. She at least doesn't go climbin' on my neck.

He found the number and began to dial. But just as he heard the receiver being lifted he dropped his own receiver on its cradle. No, that wouldn't be any good. She'd start makin' a big thing out of me not callin' her before. And you got to take a half hour coaxin' her, then she wants to stay for breakfast. Hell with her. I got to find a chick that never learned to talk.

And then abruptly he began to cry.

He lowered his forehead to the top of the desk and wept. He cried for no reason that he could remember. He had been aware of only exhaustion, a total and relentless exhaustion. But crying was something unexpected, something he would never have allowed himself to do if... If I knew what I was doin', if I had control of myself!

The sounds of his weeping fascinated and then lulled him. For a moment they were comforting and he wept until he heard footsteps. His head jerked up and he blew his nose.

Al's voice. "Joe?"

He dried his eyes and blinked heavily as if this would make any possible redness disappear. He moved the chair around. He reached for a book and pretended to concentrate on Webster's Unabridged Dictionary as Al entered.

"Joe? Busy?"

He didn't look up. He shook his head and replied, " 'Mon in."

He waited for the door to close before he shut the book and raised his head. He faced away from his brother and tried to remember what Al looked like.

"Here, Joe. Have some ginger ale." Al came around to him and offered a glass. "Clyde gave it to me."

Joey accepted the glass and closed his eyes. He felt defenseless, somehow, unable to look at Al. He was uncomfortable with him and thought of Al as the top man and himself as a small boy.

"How's it going, kid?"

"Not bad, Joe."

Joey motioned to the armchair. "Talk a minute."

Al removed his topcoat. He reached for the envelope and placed it on the desk. "What's that?" Joe asked.

"A hundred dollars."

Joe whistled through his teeth. "You're a chump."

Smiling, Al nodded and said, "You always said that about me. It won't work, Joe. I'll take money when I can earn it."

Good old Al, Joey thought, you never talk at the top of your lungs. A guy can have a conversation with you. You're a chump from 'way back, but you're O.K., baby.

"The deal's set for scorin' the show. You know that, don't ya?"

"You said this morning it would be up to someone else to decide."

Joey waved his hand. "Aaah, that was for the hicks to overhear. I say you got the job."

He sat back and folded his arms across his chest. "You got a contract out on the Coast that needs to be broken?"

"No problem."

"Awright, so you're clear. I'm bouncin' the creep we got now. He likes the booze too much. Don't worry about a thing. Musical bridges, settin' up solos, an' a little bit o' chorus work. You have a couple tunes of your own, don't ya? I don't know any songs past 'Rock of Ages,' so you can stick one or two of your own in from time to time." He paused and studied Al. "Whaddaya lookin' at?"

"You, Joe. You seem different, relaxed."

Joey chuckled. "I'm O.K., baby. It's like you're a good omen around the house. Maybe I got a little scare tonight so now I'll be a good boy. That makes sense, don't it?" He waited only until Al began to answer. He interrupted with "How'd you make out with Lory Kimball?"

"Make out?"

"You take her home?" Al nodded. "Good. I don't have to tell you, kid, she was the last twist in the world I wanted around to see that scene tonight. What'd she say about me on the way home?"

Al fooled with a cigarette. "You've got a lot of friends, Joe."

Joey chuckled and rose from the chair. He opened the door and sniffed perfume. "Clyde's got the tub ready." He returned to Al. "O.K., kid, I don't third-degree people. I got a ways to go yet with her. You don't have to play along and tell me stories. I'm gonna buckle down, sweetheart. You wait an' see, you comin' here's gonna be the best thing in life for me. You turn in if you wanna. I'm gonna take a bath an' go to sleep. I feel pretty good, ya know?"

Joe clumped out of the room, undressing as he went.

Al sat alone for a while, finishing a cigarette and lighting a second one with the ash of the first. He'd seen and talked with enough people today to send him down strange alleys. Finally he got up and went to his room. There was a kind of peace in the apartment tonight, unlike the frenetic and loud anxiety that had splashed through it last night. Joey seemed on the ball. Eye-on-the-trigger stuff. Al took his clothes off and hung his suit in the closet. Yep, there was a chance, a better than even chance, to work things out....

In the morning, Gladys brought him some coffee, the Times and two morning tabloids. He glanced over the Times headlines and then leafed idly through one of the tabloids.

At the bottom of page three, Al read:

COMIC GETS SOCKS, NOT YOCKS
AT CELEBRITY PARTY

CHAPTER EIGHT

O SBORNE COLTER rose from his bed, refreshed. He made his way to the breakfast table that stood near the balcony overlooking the river. He had had six hours of restful sleep and now he was hungry.

He reached for his orange juice.

He smelled Margot's strong cologne and heard her moving about, slamming doors with much energy. Today was her movie day.

"Such a rush, pet?"

Margot didn't answer. She hurried into her clothes and silently swore at the clock for not having wakened her.

Colter tapped at his hard-boiled egg. "I was talking, puss."

"Yes, I'm in a rush," she snapped. "I've got to see cowboys and Indians at ten o'clock.."

"What's really upsetting you?"

Margot stopped and stared at her husband. It was curious. He had never been so observant before the blindness; now he had an uncanny ability for sensing moods.

"Get Laurence to read you the morning papers," she said finally.

He chuckled. "Someone covered the party last night?"

"Covered's not the word. That foul Henry Meredith; I begged you not to invite him, Poppy! He wrote it as if we were all using hashish last night. It's the worst thing that could have happened to Joey right now."

Colter calmly stirred his coffee. "You'll have to telephone Mr. French and ask his forgiveness. Apparently you had planned a much less active evening for him." Colter waited smilingly for a reaction that didn't come. Then he continued. "Why don't you skip the cowboys and Indians and dash over to see him, pet? Say you're sorry for making a wrestler of him in your living room."

"Please, Poppy, no cat scratching so early in the morning."

"Maybe he'll ask you to stay for tea and—other entertainment."

"Poppy ... "

"But of course you'd shriek and explain you're a married woman, wouldn't you?"

"I'm leaving now, Poppy."

"How many times have you forgotten you're married, pet? A blind man would like to know for the record."

The door slammed.

Chuckling, Colter groped for his cane. He tapped his way to the phone between the twin beds and dialed Information. He asked for the number of a theatrical phone service. Then he dialed that number. Politely, he asked the woman if he might leave a message for Miss Virginia Hutch.

Joey's hands trembled as he read the article. Al stood near Joey's bed, silent, as Clyde Waverly tried to be soothing.

"Joey, don't make a Supreme Court case out of it."

Oaths flowed from Joey and he paced the room as he read, under Henry Meredith's by-line:

Comedian Joey French, known in some circles as the Million-Dollar Dynamo, last night found his wealth and energy no weapons against the bitter physical attack of an attractive, unidentified young woman.

French was a guest, along with other Broadway and Hollywood notables, including Lory Kimball and Pedro

Vez, at a party given by columnist Margot Connell and her author husband, Osborne Colter.

French had escorted Miss Kimball (the two have been called an item), and everyone was having a good time as the liquor flowed freely. The comic was in fine fettle when he entertained the crowd with material that might bewilder his TV moppet audience. Shortly after midnight, the unknown young woman barged in and hurled epithets and fists at Mr. Dynamo as she accused him of ditching their love idyl and replacing her with glamorous Lory Kimball, now portraying a lady of the evening in "Cloud Number Seven."

The television clown took his tongue-lashing and head-beating like a dutiful Casanova. But this soon gave way to a lashing of his own....

Joey ripped the newspaper in two and shouted to Clyde, "Get on the phone an' call Meredith! If he's not in his office, find him! Don't stand there, *get* him!"

Clyde wet his lips. "Do you think—"

"Goddamnit, get him on the line right away or get the hell off my payroll!" He was a raging animal, Al thought, as he moved away and watched. He'd been angry last night, too, but there had been the need for some restraint then. Now all control had vanished.

Clyde made call after call as Joey continued to pace, to kick chairs and tables that stood in his way. "Man thinks he's got a friend in the world! Who'd I ever hurt? Who'd I ever do dirt to? Where's that sonuvabitch get off writin' stuff like that? Where'd I ever do him wrong?"

Al sat and balanced a coffee cup on his knee. Joey was conscious of no one, of nothing but the pain.

"I treated him like my own!" Joey was shouting now. "I gave him news tips, I bought him a dozen hand-painted ties for

Christmas, and he called me personally to tell me thanks. They stab ya in the back! They look ya square in the kisser an' stab ya in the back!"

And then Clyde was saying, "Hold the line," and nodding to Joey. The huge man paused a moment, clutching a bedpost for support. He snapped his fingers and demanded a cigarette from Clyde. Without waiting for it, he gripped the receiver and lifted it. Al could see him shaking.

His voice was calm. "Meredith? … What kind of a question is that, how am I? I'm just dandy. How're you? … " He was quiet for what might have been a full fifteen seconds as Meredith evidently plunged into an explanation. Then, suddenly, Joey broke loose.

"Now you listen while I tell you something, you crumby tenth-rate hack: You wrote it up good so I can't sue the pants off that rotten rag of yours. But you take my warning clear now. When I see you—I don't care where it's at—I'm gonna break your goddamn head open, Meredith. You hear me now. I don't care if they toss me in the poky for life, I'm gonna split your head! You were my friend once, an' you crossed me, an' I don't let God Almighty cross me. So you keep an eye out for me for the rest of your life, when you're eatin' in a restaurant, when you're seein' a show, when you're walkin' down the street. I'll get you, Meredith!" He slammed the receiver down.

Forty minutes later Joey emerged from the bathroom, singing.

He clumped from room to room, wearing only pink shorts, drying the shaving soap from his neck. " 'Without a song—gg …' " he roared merrily. Gladys busied herself dusting furniture, and paid little attention to him.

Al, shaved and dressed, hurried from his own room. "Joe?"

"Put your socks on, sweetheart, an' show up at the Justin Theatre this afternoon, ya hear? Soak up some a the atmosphere, like they say. We'll start the dress rehearsal about four. Show's at nine."

"You all right, Joe?"

Joey grinned and threw the towel around Al's shoulders, straight and strong, once more French the Indomitable.

"I'm eighty million dollars, kid! It's like I always say: When Butch O'Dwyer goes gunnin' for ya, ya gotta gun right back or you're never gonna rest. Don't worry, kiddo." He turned to leave. On the way out, he pinched Gladys on the cheek. "I got Gladys' love to keep me warm."

"Mr. *French!*" she giggled.

Al laughed and went to the study. I'll phone Bill Kunstler, he thought; tell him to keep Phil Thompson on the show. If Joe can pull out of this morning's quicksand, he can pull out of anything.

Clyde was at the desk, using the phone. Al pantomimed willingness to leave, but Clyde shook his head.

"That's right: Kimball. K-I-M-B-A-L-L. Three dozen white roses. And write this. Uh ... 'What I do and what I dream include thee, as the wine must taste of its own grapes.' Got that? Sign it 'Joey.' J-O-E-Y. That's right. And charge it to Mr. French's account. ... Right. ... How soon'll it get there? ... Fine."

He hung up, scribbled a few words, and looked up. "Hi."

Al came closer. "Joe a poet now?"

"I'm the poet, courtesy of Elizabeth Browning. Have you seen that Kimball girl yet, by the way? Oh, that's right. You were at the free-for-all last night, weren't you? Frankly, I don't know what Joey sees in her." He rose.

"Does Joe get serious with girls very often?"

Clyde shrugged. "Nobody can look into that cavern called Joey's mind. Between you and me, I think he just wants her to prove something to himself; then he'll drop her. But don't quote me. Who knows what makes Joey tick? An hour ago, we thought he'd have apoplexy, right? Now he's singing like a kid. No, I think Joey's all right and I wouldn't take all the guff I take if I thought I was a tenth the man he was. Don't quote me."

Al nodded. Clyde rustled the inevitable papers and left the room.

Alone, Al placed his call to California. As he waited, he thought about the three dozen white roses. There seemed to be only one thing to do: forget he'd ever met Lory Kimball until she faced Joe and explained what she felt, and showed him it was a lost cause.

"Mr. William Künstler," the operator sang. "I have a call from New York City."

But, damnit, you don't meet a girl like that and forget her, Al thought. She gets in your blood fast.

"Hello, Al," came Künstler's voice.

Al explained the situation. Yeah, Bill agreed, Phil Thompson wasn't bad at all on the show. They talked on, and even before Al described his offer from Joey, Bill was telling him to do what he thought best.

He hung up, feeling like a free man. He rose, paced the room, and stood for a while, amusing himself with Joey's mint-condition library. When he could hold off no longer, he searched for Lory's phone number in the address book. He didn't know why the hell he was calling.

Lory's voice was velvet and husky. "Hello?"

You capital-J jerk, Al cursed at himself.

"Good morning," he said. "This is Elmo Lincoln."

"Al!"

"Hey, calm, calm, calm!"

"Al, this is fantastic! I dreamed about you! What's that mean?"

"You're going to take a long journey," he laughed.

"Al, how are you?"

"I'm fine, Lory. I wanted to—"

"Al, will you be around the NBC Grille at noon? I have one of those haunted-house broadcasts at two. Can I buy you lunch?"

Al paused until he thought it might be noticeable. "Twelve. A date."

"I should've told you yesterday, Al. I have a boomerang personality. It wasn't till an hour or so after you left that I looked out the window like a moon-struck goat and said, 'I *like* that man.' "

"Twelve. NBC Grille."

Crossing West 49th, Al saw Ginny Hutch's father. Al ducked instinctively into a shop vestibule. Hutch shuffled by, shoulders sagging, eyes partly closed, almost a caricature of a beaten man.

Al stared after him for a moment, then squared his own shoulders and continued to Radio City. Lory was only a minute late.

Her smile was wide and giving. She wore a smart tailored suit and a silly hat. She took Al's arm and her voice was low and happy. "I keep remembering that dream last night."

Al laughed with her and guided her to a booth. "Let's find a cozy analyst's couch and I'll interpret the dream for you."

They ordered, and Lory chattered gaily about her broadcast, about wakening suddenly from this fantastic dream in time to see the sun rise.

"It was the most beautiful sight. And all the more beautiful because it was happening in Podunk, just like in Manhattan."

"Do you know," Al said reflectively, "it's been years since I've seen a sunrise? I'm ashamed to say it."

Lory's finger traced over the veins in his hand. "It's not quite the same thing, watching it come up all by yourself. You need someone to share it."

She was looking away from Al but she was talking directly to him, telling him shyly, in a crowded restaurant, that she wanted to be loved by him.

Al raised her chin with a crooked finger. "Lory . .

She looked at him and nodded.

"I love you, Lory."

"No, let's not say it yet, Alan. Let's not make any pacts. Let's just ... see each other."

"Beginning tonight."

Lory nodded. "I'll be through at the theatre at half past eleven. Will you meet me there?"

Al said quietly, "With a pound and a half of hamburger under my arm."

CHAPTER NINE

A L LEFT RADIO CITY at a quarter past one and headed for the
Rockland Broadcasting System, over on Fifth. He walked
quickly, not because he felt a responsibility to Joey or the new
job, but simply because he felt happy for the first time in-how
long? he wondered; certainly not for a year. Happiness had been
an elusive thing since his wife's death. There had been a minor
pride now and then in the KJK job. He'd forgotten his emptiness
for hours when he'd opened a bottle with some of the Malibu
Beach gang. There had been occasional girls, never important.
He'd forgotten how good happiness could taste. Lory.

She had told him a great deal about herself in that crowded
restaurant. She'd told about her two-year marriage to a painter,
which had ended in his suicide. She'd told him about her guilt
that had lasted a year, for not being sorry he was dead. She'd
described her indecisions, doubts of love and work and the city.
But always she had been animated, alive, talking to *him*. And, in
kind, he had opened up and told her what Louise had meant to
him and what he thought he wanted to achieve.

All within something like seventy minutes, he thought now
as he walked just a trifle more slowly. And within seventy minutes, neither of us mentioned Joe....

The RBS sign was two blocks up. He glanced at his watch:
one-thirty-nine. The breeze had freshened into a wind within the
last few minutes and Al turned his coat collar up. Imperceptibly
the sky had darkened, and movement on the streets about him

became faster. By the time he got to the RBS building he was running, for rain had begun to beat down mercilessly, like a breath too long held. He dashed into the lobby.

Ginny Hutch was there.

She saw him come in, wiping the rain from his forehead. She moved to him as though she'd been expecting him. Anxiety clouded her pretty face, her hair was only partly combed, and Al saw snags in her stockings. But it was hard for him to forfeit happiness, and he found himself smiling. This is Hutch Day, he thought.

"Hello, Al," Ginny said. Her voice was small. She looked lost in this gigantic first floor, a well-developed child wearing too much make-up.

"Hello, Ginny. You the new doorman here?"

"Can I talk to you, Al?"

He raised his eyebrows and nodded. He saw a tweed-covered couch near the elevator and led her to it. She sat with an elderly-lady thud, and he sat beside her, offering her a cigarette. She took one but stared down at the marble floor.

He said nothing until she found the courage to look at him. "Al, you're my friend, aren't you?"

"I hope so, Ginny."

"You know I had eyes for you from the very first time we met, no matter what Joey would've thought, don't you?"

The little-girl plea in her voice moved Al, and he had to refocus his view of her to remind himself that she was the young hellion who had caused all the ruckus last night.

"That's nice to hear, Ginny. Honest. What's wrong?"

She took his hand. "Al, take me upstairs with you."

His eyes narrowed. "Have you been up?" he asked, knowing the answer.

"They won't let me in. All I want is to see him, Al, that's all. What's so wrong with that? If you take me and say you're Joey French's *brother* and take my hand when you walk in, why, nobody's gonna say nothing."

"What are you looking for, Ginny? What do you want with Joe?"

She stared down at the marble floor again. "I just want to see what's going on between he and I."

Al made his voice gentle. "You're on the ball, Ginny. You must know."

She shook her head. "I don't know."

"He was pretty rough last night. What does that usually mean?"

Ginny looked at him. "I know Joey two months. More! He's been rough, sure, plenty of times. I just have to know what's about now, Al. I don't want to cause any hassels, honest. If Joey says sure, come back, I'll run. You hear how I'm talking, Al? I'll run! But this dumb bellboy upstairs, I tell him my name, that I want to go in, and he goes around asking questions, and he comes back and says no. Al, I'm not twelve years old. I couldn't sleep all night long. I've got to know. Nobody's gonna push me around."

"Ginny, let's face it. What do you want from Joey? What do you expect to get from him?"

"He's a big star."

"With problems, Ginny. You're a fine kid and he's a great guy, but you'll do better to look for someone else."

She edged away and frowned. "I didn't ask for your advice. I don't have to take advice from anybody."

Al got up. "See you around, huh?"

"They're gonna put me on the cover of Life!"

"So long, Ginny."

"Al, don't leave me here!" Ginny grasped at his coat. Irritation grew in him and he had to get away from her.

"Listen to me," he said firmly. "We can play this record over a hundred times but it's still going to add up to the same thing. Joe made a mistake the first time he said a few nice words to you. You're in his hair now, kid. You're in everybody's hair. So beat it and find yourself another boy. And stay away from Joe."

Al turned and walked quickly to the elevator, hoping she wouldn't follow. She didn't. From the corner of his eye he could see her weave for a moment, then pick up her coat and go to a phone booth near the newsstand. Poor daffy kid, he thought; but I'm damned if I'll cry in my beer over her.

He asked for the Joey French rehearsal. All the way up to the twentieth floor the clear image of Lory occupied his thoughts. He remembered that he was happy.

Joey was cursing an electrician as Al entered the studio, but neither the electrician nor anyone else seemed particularly upset. There were perhaps forty people on stage and scattered through the audience seats, most of them paying rapt attention to Joey, who held center stage. Al shrugged out of his coat, eyes on his brother. He heard, "Alan! Ssst!" hoarsely whispered from somewhere, and he looked around to find Don Haven in the second row.

Don was wearing a vehemently blue cardigan jacket with a plaid sports shirt. He winked and patted the seat beside him as Al approached "Hi, Alan. Meet Tony." Al looked past Don to nod to an older and fastidiously clean man who nodded back. "Alan's Joey's brother," Don explained.

"Swell!" Tony said.

" Joey's yelling blue murder today," Don told Al. "Everything going wrong, he thinks. But then he's always this way before a performance."

From the stage, Joey turned and faced Don squarely. He shouted, "Who the hell's doin' all that yak-yak-yak? Ya wanna talk, go outside an' talk. Let a man hear himself think around here, will ya?"

And as quickly, he turned back to the electrician. Don's face reddened.

Al was impressed with what he saw. Not one person on stage was unaware of Joey, who paced the stage noisily, carrying a large glass of milk. He wore a striped polo shirt and his paunch showed. He was finishing his lecture to the electrician but his eyes traveled the length and breadth of the stage with omniscience. "Awright, Frank," he ended, letting his voice fall slightly, "you know I don't mean anything by what I say. Just keep the eye on the ball, yeah?"

"Right, Mr. French."

"Good boy. Awright, Spider, ya ready for Helene's number now? An' for Pete's sakes, let's everybody wake up here! We're not puttin' on 'Craig's Wife' in the Methodist church tonight!"

Joey was keyed up, intense, driving with dedicated passion. Within the next hour he insulted a dozen people, from the script girl to Helene Brenner, the Hollywood singer and guest star this week; he directed scenes that included him and those that did not; he changed from nagging bully to likable clown and back to bully again with rhythmic ease. It was quite a performance, Al thought.

Joey dismissed the cast at three o'clock for an hour's break, but he continued to work, checking costumes, listening to music, giving orders to the grip men. Al rose, excused himself from Don and Tony, and walked to the back of the theatre. Margot Connell, sitting in the last row, smiled.

"Don't we keep bumping into each other, though?"

Al sat and accepted a sip from the coffee container she offered him. "You escaping last night's notoriety?" he asked.

"Oh, that! That's forgotten. I'm just here watching a genius at work."

Al nodded. "He's a real maestro, isn't he?"

"I think these few days have done wonders for him, Al. Last night didn't mean a thing; after a few minutes he was our Joey again. I mean, in general, he seems more ... paced, is that the word? Is it just coincidental that it started when you came to town?"

"Me? I haven't said more than thirty words to Joey in three days. If Joe's in good form it's because of Joe."

"Maybe it's your sobering influence. He and I were talking around one o'clock today. He told me he feels strong and healthy and he praised you to the skies."

Al laughed. "Good Lord, I keep hearing Joe's press-agenting me. What for? What've I done to deserve all this?"

Margot finished her coffee and dropped a cigarette butt in the container. She swirled it around and looked at it reflectively. "Joey's a complicated animal. He tears the rafters down when he learns someone he's trusted is working against him. Whether you know it or not—and whether he knows it or not—Joey's made something holy of you, Al. He's convinced he can always count on you never to let him down." Her voice took on a toneless quality. "I hope all that faith is justified, Al."

Al frowned and faced her. "Margot, what are you getting at?"

"Lory Kimball. What's between you two?"

"For your column?"

"For Joey. I want to know for Joey's sake. I don't want to see him hurt."

"She's not his property, is she?"

Margot shook her head. "No, and it's obvious she never will be. But whether he realizes that or not yet isn't important. I don't think he's seen her more than once or twice, but he's been mapping out a love affair with her for the past two months, in the way a general maps out a frontal attack. I told you he's complicated. When he sees something he wants, he's got to have it, and reason be damned. Al, stay away from her. For a while, anyway. He won't suffer so much if she keeps on ignoring him. After a little he'll convince himself that *he* did the jilting."

This was neither new nor startling, Al thought. This had always been Joe's pattern, quietly but doggedly pursuing the unreachable. Like when he was delivering groceries by day and seeking out important actresses at night to tell them they didn't know him but he was a millionaire from Texas and how would they like to invite him up to their apartments? They would evade

COME FEED ON ME

him or laugh at him and this treatment would genuinely bewilder Joe.

"Did you hear me, Al?"

"I heard you, Margot. Thanks for the tip."

He heard Joe bellowing from the stage. "Al! Hey, Al, you there? 'Mere a minute. Wanna see ya."

Al walked down the aisle. Joey still held the glass of milk, the fingers of his free hand dug into his slacks pocket. He was talking with a small, bespectacled man as Al ascended the stage.

"Kiddo," Joey said, "wanna have ya meet Jack Gallagher, the producer of this hoedown. Jack, this's Al, the kid brother."

They shook hands. "Have a minute, Al?" Gallagher asked. "We can go back to Joey's dressing room and have a chat."

"Yeah," Joey said, and began to move toward someone who was calling him. "Take 'im back 'an show 'im how to make one of those bow ties so he can teach me. Awright, Nate, I'm cornin'."

In the dressing room Gallagher mentioned Joey's suggestion about Al's taking over as music director. He asked Al several questions and Al answered clearly. They talked for twenty minutes and then Gallagher produced some manuscripts of past shows for Al to study.

"I'm sure we can work out something, Al. Joey, you know, is your A-one rooter. Thinks you're tops. Responsible, creative; there's always room for that in show business. Well, let's get back to Siberia, what do you say?"

Al sat through the dress rehearsal, and felt Don Haven's eyes on him. At half past six Joey called, " 'Mon along to eat, Al." He accompanied Joe, three men, and two women to a dairy restaurant, but didn't exchange a word with Joe throughout the meal. Joe talked constantly. He seemed relaxed and in excellent spirits.

Al watched the 'how from the control room. Each time Joe got a laugh, Al glanced at the controls that reported the sound reaction. There were a lot of laughs.

At the end of the show he went on stage and said hello to Clyde Waverley. Clyde explained that Joey and a gang were on their way to a bop session up in the Eighties. Would Al like to come along? "No, thanks, Clyde. Another time," Al said, and remembered suddenly it was too late to buy hamburger.

He left the studio and walked to the West Side hurriedly. The rain had stopped but a heaviness had taken over the city air. Al slackened his pace, then abruptly stepped into a Sixth Avenue bar. He drank slowly until the hands of the wall clock inched their way to eleven.

He stood at the stage door of the Strauss and searched his pockets for a cigarette. He went to the corner, bought a pack, and went back again, feeling all the while that it was nonsense to remember Margot Connell's words. But he was uneasy.

He took up his vigil at the stage door, watching the cast stream by him. Lory was probably the last one out of the theatre. She wore a simple sweater and skirt under her coat, and she hastened to Al.

"I never thought I'd be a stage-door Johnny," he said, feeling the pressure of her hand in his.

Lory grinned and they walked to Eighth Avenue and a taxi. "I'm sorry, Al. I should have invited you in to see the show. But it's such a piece of junk."

"I saw it. Yesterday matinee."

"No!" she cried. They got into the cab and she gave the address. She turned to him and reached for his hand. "Why didn't you tell me? I'm so ashamed."

"Of this play? Don't be silly."

"Angry, I mean. I used to play Saint Joan and Portia and Laura Wingfield and I couldn't even get the charwomen in to see me. Now I'm in this thing that I'd give my right arm to get out of, and *everybody* sees it. Yesterday's matinee? Gosh, that second act yesterday was—"

He kissed her, and he knew she could hear his heart beating.

The delicatessen next door was still open when they got to Houston Street. Al asked her if she'd accept hot pastrami instead of hamburger. She nodded and told him to go ahead. She would be upstairs, heating the broiler and emptying ash trays.

She walked to the vestibule and he watched her go before he turned in at the store.

CHAPTER TEN

"LOVE ME, darling," Lory whispered.

The pastrami and accessories lay untouched on the refrigerator. She and Al held one another tenderly, and then passionately and then tenderly again, feeling wonderfully alive.

They said damn and damnation later when they looked for cigarettes and found none. Then Al remembered he had a pack in his coat. Lory leaped up and walked to the other room. In the darkness he could see the clean outline of her body, with her long, slim legs. She returned with the pack, lit two cigarettes, and gave him one. They began their second cigarettes without having spoken. This was good, Al thought; at a time like this she was intuitive enough to be silent.

When his arm began to cramp, he gently ordered, "Move!" and she raised her head. He kissed her again.

"What have you been thinking?" she asked.

"You. I love you."

"So fast?"

"Um, and I'm usually such a slow-moving gent."

"I'm glad, Alan. Very glad."

"You say that with such holiness."

"I know. Because I mean it. I started out hoping we wouldn't get past the hello, how are you stage, because love is such a fearsome thing to me and I'm scared of it. How can I say it? I'm more impressed now with being loved than by being loved by you. Is that confusing?"

Al shook his Lead. "No. Everyone expects love to be very tidy and pat, but it never is. Don't worry. And don't try to analyze it. We'll last a lot longer if we just let love take the old natural course."

"I'm a very sentimental-type girl, Alan. But not ... impulsive. I ... wanted you to know that. Alan ... "

"Um?"

"I don't want to sound like a nagging wife, but what are you thinking about?"

"Joe."

"Why?"

Al remembered the first thing he'd noticed in the apartment tonight: three dozen white roses.

"Because not any of the three of us deserves a kick in the jaw, Lory. Joe's got to understand that you're the free agent you say you are because you simply don't want him. Not because of me."

He felt her stiffen.

"You don't agree?"

Lory said it slowly. "Alan, if we're going to go on after today, there's one thing you've got to do for me. You've got to be a man. I was married once. I was married to a Greek god. Every time I looked at him I thought he'd just stepped off a Parthenon frieze. But he was weak and drunken and passive, and I can't live with that any more. It's got to be better this time, or it's got to be nothing at all."

Al took her arm and made her face him. "Lory, I'll work hard to make things come out the right way. But I won't let you put me on trial."

Lory smiled meekly. "No more talk?"

He smiled back and shook his head.

"How about the hot pastrami?"

"Soon," he answered.

In the front room of Nora Burchill's West Side apartment the party was in full swing. For the past five minutes the guests—most of whom were musicians—had been involved in an elaborate interpretation of "One O'clock Jump." Now they were moving to an off-chord inspection of "Why Can't You Behave?" Here, in the back room, Nora lounged on the couch as Joey paced with increasing frenzy. Nora watched him silently. He had appeared an hour ago, riding on top of the world. Then, from nowhere, he'd become vicious, wild.

The music reached a piercing crescendo and Joey hunched his shoulders.

"What's with me, Nora? I'm failin' apart. I'm shakin' like Jello. What happened that I'm actin' like some crazy mutt?"

"Get on some alcohol rub, Joey," she said, and rose to pour a drink for him.

He shook his head and fell to the chair opposite her. "I don't want booze. I'm sick! I never felt so shaky! The show went good, everything was perfect. I came here feelin' great. But now I'm shakin' like a kid! What's it mean? Out o' nowhere, I tell ya!"

Through the barbarous music they heard the telephone. Nora looked to the door. Joey's attention fixed on her and he struggled to stop trembling. He could feel sweat fixing his undershirt to his chest.

"Nora!" somebody called. "Pick up!"

Nora excused herself, leaving him alone. He got up and began to follow her, afraid of staying here by himself, although all three lights were on. Get a hold, get a hold! he thought. Don't give in, don't make a baby out of yourself, don't crack....

She returned, bunching the folds of her robe together. "Ginny," she said.

"No, no, no! Say I'm not here!"

Nora nodded. "I dug it. I told her you cut out an hour ago. She's cornin' over, though."

Joey began to tie his necktie with shaking fingers. "I'll go, Nora. I don't want to see her. Tell everyone, ya understand? I was here for just a second and I left. I went outta town. Tell 'er I went outta town."

"Why not face her, Joey? She's just a kid; she can't hurt you."

Joey brought his coat around his shoulders, still shaking his head. "I'll be awright, soon's I get some fresh air. Just need some air."

Nora stood on her toes and kissed him lightly on the cheek. "Cut out, man, and dig yourself. Relax."

He nodded desperately and hurried out the side door. Herb was waiting in the car. Joey darted into the back seat and rasped, "Home. Fast. Make it fast."

He buttoned his coat collar and shivered, choking back the tears.

He hastened to his bedroom and searched for the thermometer. He had begun to feel less tense and weak as the car had headed for home, but now he sat on his bed and placed the thermometer under his tongue, trying to prepare himself for bad news. I'll fight this, he thought. I won't give in.

The temperature was surprisingly normal and he laughed. He took off all his clothes and barked for Clyde. But then he remembered that Clyde was still at the ball with the rest of the gang. Hell with it, he told himself, and headed for the bathroom; I'm no kid. He let the tub water run. He heard the phone ring and it startled him. He answered it. The instant he heard Ginny's voice he hung up. He returned to the bathroom and reached for the wine-red robe on the floor. The phone rang again. He turned the water off and stood near the tub, listening to the persistent rings. He lit a cigarette and watched his hand shake. He pitched the cigarette into the tub and moved swiftly to the phone.

"Hello!" he bellowed.

"Joey, wudja hang up on me for?"

"Because I wantcha to keep away from me, ya hear? We're through, done, over. I don't like ya crossin' me. I don't like anybody crossin' me. Now keep away, kid."

"How'd I cross you, Joey? Tell me how, Joey. Don't get sore."

"I'm warnin' you one thing: I see you again, I'll bust your throat. Ya need a buck, gimme your address, I'll send ya a check."

"Whaddaya think I am?"

"A bum. Ya want the check or no? Quick, kid."

"Joey, you'll pay for making a laughingstock out of me!"

"Get lost," he said, and hung up. He chuckled. I'm really blowin' my cork, that I'd let a nothin' like that eat me up alive! What'm I so jumpy about? Over a nothing like her?

He swaggered to the study, suddenly remembering the bulging brief case of papers that Clyde had been asking him to look at. He switched on lights as he walked and chuckled again as the phone began to ring. He got the brief case and brought it back to the card table in his bedroom. He went to the kitchen and poured some ginger ale. He imitated the sound of the telephone that kept ringing. He returned to the bedroom, ready to work through the night if necessary.

He switched the radio on and lowered himself to a chair. Suddenly pain shot through his head. He staggered and pressed the hot palm of a hand against his forehead, determined to wait a moment, relax, until the pain went away. His legs trembled and he leaned hard against the closet. In a moment he could breathe evenly and there was only a hint of an ache in his head. He smiled; he had won. He sat at the table and began to go through the papers. The phone rang again. He ignored it. A remote churning began in his stomach. He took a long, sighing drag on the cigarette he didn't remember having lighted. The print on the paper blurred.

The ring of the phone was piercing. He stood up and lunged for it. "Get *off!* Get *off!* Get *off!*" he shouted. "Hang up! Get off!" He slapped the receiver down. He paced and remembered Jean Bixby. "I'll call Jean," he said aloud. "I'll tell her to run over. Have a couple laughs."

He telephoned and said, "Make it snappy." He returned to the table and sat. A not unpleasant tingling sensation darted through his lips and he felt a dryness in his throat. Lemme get in bed, he thought. The hell with the work. I'll lay down for a minute an' wait for Jean. I'll let this pass....

The chair scraped back and, from the tail of his eye, as he staggered to his bed, he saw that he had overturned the card table. The papers were strewn on the floor. A violent constriction tore through his stomach and he stood erect, fighting, fighting it off, passionately eager to win again. He tried to get to the bathroom, but he tripped and fell. His shoulder scraped against the bureau as he dropped to the floor, trying to speak, to call for help, and trying still to see this through himself. One hand clenched around a bureau leg and the other pounded the floor in fright, in anger, in helpless frustration.

He was suddenly aware that he had hurt his shoulder; he felt its throb ticking rhythmically. He was able to concentrate on it and this satisfied him. I fell, that's all, he said to himself, I fell and hit my shoulder. Happens every day, happens to everyone. Where do I get off makin' such a fuss?

Immediately he felt a return of strength and again he smiled; or did he laugh aloud? He'd beaten it. He hadn't given in. Give in, give in, give in an' you're dead.... Give in, give in, give in an' they got ya, you're not worth the powder to blow ya up....

He gradually lifted himself to his feet. He heard the phone from a distance. He moved his hand in the direction of the doorknob when suddenly he was unable to see the light, to find it. A glittering haze circled in front of him and he saw only the swirl of neat and patterned dots.

He fell once more. As he descended into semiconsciousness he thought about his robe, something about his robe, something, something, damn robe, just bought it, ruined it, got to throw it away, damn robe....

He awoke with a sudden rush of clarity. The phone was still ringing. And so was the doorbell.

Joey took the receiver off the hook and wondered why he hadn't thought of that before. He leaned against the wall for a moment and worked to pull himself together. "Just a minute!" he called to the impatient buzzer.

He walked unsteadily to the door. Good old Jean, he thought; she always comes through. He would have to excuse himself, tell her to fix a drink while he washed his face and snapped back into commission. He opened the door.

Don Haven stood in the vestibule, alone.

Joey frowned. Don took a tentative step forward, smiling. "Joey! You look like you lost your last friend!"

"Don?"

"You really had me worried, you know that, Joey? I've been standing out here at least three or four minutes."

"Where do you— How come—"

"What's wrong? You act as though you expected someone else. Say, I don't want to stand in this vestibule all night, pretty as it is."

Joey moved back and admitted him. "Uh—sorry. 'Mon in."

He closed the door and Don moved past him, unwinding a yellow scarf. "Call that speed," he said. "I was just dipping into a new edition of Rimbaud when you called and told me to hustle over here. Joey, I'm really worried. You don't look at all well."

"I called you?"

"Have you been flirting with John Barleycorn?"

"When'd I call? I— It slipped my mind."

"Why, twenty minutes ago. Now, are you going to hang up this coat like a good fellow or do you want me to go stomping out of here?"

"Uh—yeah. Gimme the coat. Oh—uh—go in an' make yourself a drink. I'll be with you in a couple minutes."

Joey started down the hall. He heard a phone ringing from the living room and called, "Don't answer that. Just take it off the hook, will ya?"

Don called back, "Right-o."

Crazy, foolish stunt, Joey thought. He clumped into the bedroom and put the receiver back. He lifted it, heard the hum, and dialed Jean Bixby's number. Where the hell was my head? Wadda I want with that type of guy? "H'lo, Jean?"

"Joey? This is one sweet time to call me, you big moose. How are you, sweetie?"

"How are ya, princess? Gettin' much needlework done lately?"

"You're a panic, Sabu. No, I'm sitting around waiting day in and day out for you to ring me up. I thought you were madly in love with me."

"I am, princess. Listen, there's somebody at the door. I'll buzz you tomorra, O.K.?"

"Joey, you crackpot—"

He hung up. He stood hunched, indecisive, until he heard the phone ring again. He put the receiver on its side and headed for the bathroom. He showered in icecold water, rubbed himself with a harsh towel, put on a new robe, and went to Don Haven.

"That's an awfully striking Utrillo," Don said, pointing to it. "I confess I'd underestimated your taste in art."

Joey waved his hand and picked up the drink Don had made for him. "I get a guy in here, hire him to furnish the place. Colors, decorating, the works. I don't know— What's his name?"

"Utrillo?"

"I don't know Utrillo from Petrillo." Joey moved impatiently about the room, keeping his eyes away from Haven. "Yeah. What'd you want here, Don?"

"I? *You* asked *me* over, Joey. I assumed it was about the show."

Joey nodded and sat heavily. "Oh."

"That was it, wasn't it?"

"What time is it, Don?"

"You seem occupied, Joey."

"Little jumpy."

"Tense?" Joey nodded. "Mmm, I've got something that'll knock that right out of you." Joey looked up accusingly. "A massage," Don explained. "My friend Tony taught it to me. It relaxes certain neck and back muscles. Shall I show you what it's like?"

Joey stared glumly at the Utrillo. Finally he said, "O.K."

Don leaped up and set the drink beside him. "Swell. Just collapse the old body on this couch and Dr. Haven will go to work at the union minimum."

Joey lay on the couch.

"Now just pretend you're sinking, sinking, sinking into this sofa."

Within minutes he began to feel relaxed, and it surprised him that Don's hands were so strong.

"How's it feel, Joey?"

Joey nodded.

"Want to talk about anything? The show? Anything at all? It's only fair, Joey. I thought you called me over to discuss the show. All right, turn over now."

"Yeah." He moved his huge bulk around and let Don's palms rub into his shoulder blades. "Tell ya the truth, Don, I can't think straight these days about many things. Damn kid's on my neck every minute, don't let me rest."

"Who? Alan?"

"The kid, I said. Ginny. Ginny Hutch."

"Oh."

"That's the kind of a tramp can make a man's life hell."

"Slip her a hundred dollars. Tell her to drop dead."

Joey shook his head. "Uh-uh. That's the kind takes special care. Ya either get outta town or you keep payin' through the nose."

"Or you kill her," Don laughed.

Joey was still for an instant. Then he nodded. "Or ya kill 'er."

"I've seen the likes of her," Don said. "That doesn't sound like a bad idea."

CHAPTER ELEVEN

A T BREAKFAST the next morning Al asked Clyde about Joe's schedule for the day. Sometime today, Al thought, I've got to put it on the line to him.

"Oh, Joey's in Connecticut by now," Clyde said.

"Connecticut?"

Clyde motioned to Rose for more coffee. "Very mysterious doings. I was at home sleeping when he phoned me around six this morning. He told me Herb was driving him and a few friends up to the cottage for a day or so. Told me to contact Bucky Ahearne and Jack Gallagher and excuse him for the week end."

"That's pretty sudden, isn't it?"

"For Joey, very sudden. He behaves as if he doesn't know what he'll do in the next five minutes, but actually he thinks like a calendar, plans weeks ahead. But this dropping out of sight must have been a very quick decision. Well, he needs it. A day or two at his place up there does wonders for him."

Al sipped at his coffee. He wondered why he never felt quite at ease with Waverley; there was something robot-like about Clyde. "What about the show?" he asked. "Can he take off, just like that?"

Clyde laughed and rose. "Oh, the show's no problem. Joey works out thirty-six basic formats before the season begins. The writers follow it, Bucky lines up the cast, Gallagher puts a script in all the cast's hands, and Joey shows up to conquer. He doesn't go on stage himself until the Monday before the show. I do wish there was some way for us to contact him, though. He won't have a telephone up there. Oops, that's the phone. Excuse me. Good coffee, Rose."

Al waited and tried to decide his next move. He had looked over Mike Everett's music score last night in bed. He would be able, he was convinced, to take on the job at any time. But Joe hadn't named a specific date, nor had Gallagher. Maybe I wait, he thought, like in the Air Force. Joe's giving himself some therapy on his own by taking a rest, so I'll hold tight until I hear from him.

He went into the study and dialed Lory's number. Her voice was husky and disgruntled.

"Sorry I wakened you, baby," Al said. "I just wanted to know whose little girl are you?"

"Ughhh," she said. "What time is it?"

"Quarter of eleven. I love you."

"Ughh."

"Is that a comment?"

"Good morning, Alan. Good morning, darling."

"That's better."

"You know why I'm angry? Your big vulgar brother."

Al frowned. "Come again?"

"Were you with him at exactly five-thirty-five this morning? That's when he phoned me."

"I was asleep."

"At precisely five-thirty-five. He was roaring, fallendown drunk."

Al sat up. "You're awake, aren't you, Lory? This isn't part of your dream?"

"Fully awake. He said he had some *pals*"—she pronounced it as if it were a swear word—"with him and how would it be if he took a ride over here with them and we could all have a hot time in the old town? Alan, tell me: For this kind of adolescent humor he makes fifty million dollars a year?"

"Lory, I'm sorry. Joe's not a drinker. Are you sure it was Joe? Maybe some idiot who impersonated him. Read the gossip columns and just—"

"Well, whoever it was, I let him have it. Maybe I was brutal, but he sounded so drunk and so disgusting."

Al felt a dull pressure in his stomach. "He didn't call again?"

"Once was enough. The last thing he mentioned was Connecticut. He told me about a cottage he has in Garland and why didn't I be a good scout and go with them?" Lory's sharpness drained and she seemed to sense his tension. "Alan, is anything wrong?"

"I hope not, honey. I don't know. Are you free today? Let's have lunch or dinner."

They made a date for five-thirty and he felt the quality of their affection when she whispered something gentle, just before they said good-by.

Al spent the afternoon at Ahearne's office watching kinescopes of the show and listening to music playbacks. He phoned Clyde at five to check on the news. Clyde had nothing to report. He sat through Lory's show that evening and then took her home. At noon the next day he phoned Clyde again from Lory's living room. Clyde said pleasantly, "What's all this concern, Al? You sound like an expectant father. This isn't the first time Joey's taken a sabbatical. If anything happened, we'd hear soon enough."

Lory and Al had breakfast in her kitchenette and he took her to her Saturday matinee. Except for hours away from him at the theatre, they were together through the week end. It was a solemn, tender, frequently gay, and more frequently worried week end. At nine o'clock Sunday he telephoned again. Clyde answered and his voice was strange.

"Clyde, what is it?"

"I'm glad you called, Al. Maybe it would be a good idea to hop over."

"I said what is it?"

Clyde spoke close to the mouthpiece. "He got in ten, fifteen minutes ago. He's in a bad way; never saw him like this. He brought a bunch of .weird-looking characters with him and he's in a bad way."

Before the elevator door opened, Al could hear ugly laughter coming from Joe's vestibule. It was unrestrained and yet curiously fearful laughter.

The elevator door opened and Al almost walked into two effeminate-looking men, whose laughter stopped abruptly. Al immediately recognized one of them as Tony, the older man who had sat with Haven at Joey's rehearsal.

Tony's eyes lit up for an instant as if he were about to greet Al, but just as quickly his eyes lowered in an amused kind of shame. He guided his companion into the elevator, the door closed, and Al was alone in the vestibule.

Oh, no, he thought. Don't blow your top altogether, Joe. He tried the door. It was unlocked and he went in.

He closed it quietly and turned to see Clyde approaching.

"He's in the living room," Clyde whispered. "He won't say a word. He looks as if he's been in an alley fight. To tell you the truth, I'm afraid to go near him."

"Who were those gardenias who just left?"

"Never saw them before. He brought them here for a drink. Or Don Haven brought them, I don't know which. Do you know Haven?"

"Is he here, too?"

Clyde nodded. "I don't know what to think, Al. I've seen Joey on lots of crazy kicks, but never this. You're his brother. You take over. Honest to God, I've never seen him like this!"

Al dropped his coat over Clyde's arm and moved to the living-room landing. He recognized a Muggsy Spanier record, wild and unrestrained.

Don Haven was huddled over the phonograph. He gave no evidence that he'd heard anyone come in. Joe was sitting erect in the far armchair.

Al stood in pious horror.

Joey's eyes were open but his stare was stony, vacant. A great purple bruise surrounded one eye. The other eye was puffed into distortion. All the wrinkles and sharp lines that had hidden in his huge and friendly face were apparent now as a kind of warning of his dissipation. His body was stiff, unmoving. His hands hung limply over the sides of the chair.

Al moved farther into the partially lighted room. Joey did not stir. Don looked up and grinned. "Well, welcome home, stranger!" he called in a patronizing voice. Al went to his brother.

"Joey," Don said, putting a stack of records down. "It's Alan. Remember Alan?"

"Joe," Al said softly. "Joe, what is it?"

Joe's eyes lifted. His expression did not change but his eyes fastened onto Al and stayed there.

"In so soon, Alan?" Don poised his glass near his lips. "Tell me, how could the delightful Miss Kimball bear to let you go?" Al glanced sharply at Don, who nodded. "Oh, yes, it's a coast-to-coast scandal by now. I've known about you two for a few days now, but I didn't want to spoil Joey's vacation. I saved it as a friendly *coup de grace* until we were halfway home."

Al felt a hand on his lapel. He turned to look at his brother. Joey was holding him by the coat and lifting the free hand into a fist. "Joe!"

As the Spanier record ended and a new one dropped to replace it, Joey's strength brought Al down, down until Al had collapsed to his knees. With the open palm of his other hand Joey began hitting Al's ear with unappeasable fury.

The new record began. It was pensive and mellow.

"Joe! For God's sake!" Al cried hoarsely.

Slowly Joey sat forward, still grasping Al's coat. He rose and pulled Al with him.

When he spoke his voice was strained. "Ya crossin' me, huh?"

"Joe, cut it out!" Al cried.

There was a second's pause and the grip lessened. But then he stood straight and tall and sent his fist crashing into Al's jaw. "Ya cross me, huh?"

Al lay on the floor and struggled to move away as he saw Joe's foot rise. "Joe! Joe!" Al pleaded. "Stop!"

Don Haven tried to restrain Joe, tried to pull him back. "Joey, that's no good. Please don't—"

An animal roar erupted from Joe and he shoved Haven away. His hand came down and he yanked Al to his feet. His face was frenzied now and his body shivered with hatred. He shook Al and pushed him back with jarring force. He advanced as Al fell against the sofa and then to the floor.

"Cross me, huh? Ya cross me! I'll kill ya, ya rotten sonuvabitch! Get up! Get up and I'll *kill* ya!"

Al stumbled, trying to escape. Again he felt the hand grip his lapel, jerk him up, and push him back. Clyde appeared from somewhere and stood motionless at the living-room landing.

"I give ya everything! I give ya the keys to the city an' ya cross me! Nobody crosses Joey French! Get up an' get the hell outta here! I don' wanna see ya here again! Get out!"

He half led, half dragged Al through the room to the foyer and to the door, past Haven, past the vaguely protesting Clyde. He opened the door and threw Al into the vestibule and against the elevator.

"I trusted ya! I give ya everything! No more, ya crumby two-bit jerk! Get out an' keep away!" He wheeled around and slammed the door.

Al lay still. Gradually he raised himself, tasting the blood on his lip.

On Wednesday, three mornings later, Al picked up a Broadway column and read:

What video clown
Is doing the town
With a lad who wears a lavender gown?

Al stood up and gazed out the hotel window. Indian summer would probably linger through most of the fall, he thought. The sky today was a clear, shining blue, and what clouds there were fluffed themselves across it with casual gaiety.

He had been a busy man these past days. He had registered at a small, inexpensive hotel near Sixth Avenue. He had phoned Clyde and, being told that Joey had plunged into this week's show with grim determination, Al asked that his stuff be sent here. He had wired Bill Kunstler for the salary owed him; it would be enough to tide him over for a few weeks. He had reported Joe's behavior to Dr. Haskill, but he had purposely kept away from Bucky Ahearne and from the studio. He had asked Lory if she could recommend a singer who would make some audition recordings of a few of his songs. Lory directed him to a brunette named Anne and, for five dollars, Anne met him at a recording studio to sing four songs as he played the piano. He had taken the four records to four music publishers and placed three of them to be considered. Within the next day or so, he'd been told, they would have a decision.

As he walked through the streets, he felt defeated. Each time the image of Joe came into his head he saw the picture of a man drowning.

It helped a little that Lory's play was to close this Saturday night. There would be more time for them together. And less time for me to think about how I've let him down, he thought.

He continued to move through the city with moody aimlessness. And in company with his pain and loss was a shadow that faltered behind him. He hoped it was faith in himself.

At exactly nine-forty-three on Thursday evening, Camera 2 focused on four scantily dressed girls. They were sitting in a dog sled and the North Pole snow was beating ruthlessly down from a filter above the stage. A half-dozen dogs were inching the sled forward and the studio audience laughed and waited for their chance to wave at the cameras.

Camera 1 panned with Joey French as he left the wings and approached the dog sled. He wore an enormous raccoon coat, a sombrero, and ear muffs. The audience automatically applauded, although he had appeared in three sketches tonight before this one.

" 'Taint no fit night for man nor my sponsor!" he bellowed, and flapped his hands together like a seal. In the control room two men stood near the wall. One said worriedly, "I can't put my finger on it, but he's acting sort of strange." The other man shook his head. "Take it easy. He's all right."

The audience laughed again, and louder, as the clown removed his coat with elegance and dropped it to the floor. He was wearing an old-fashioned striped bathing suit. "Ah-hah! What have we here?" he shouted, seeing the girls and waddling to them. "Now I see why the nights are six months long. Ah-hah-hah-hah!"

The cue was picked up and the music began for Joey's solo, "Let's Rub Noses." As he sang he helped the girls, one by one, off the sled. The impudent, pixie grin was still on his face but, one of the girls discovered, his palms were deathly cold and his legs were trembling.

"It'll be easy sleddin' for us in this snow,
So let's rub noses, my pretty little Eskimo...".

The last of the four girls raised her leg to be helped out of the sled. She tripped and only for an instant lost her balance, but Joey made an elaborate affair of helping her up and dusting her. One of the men in the control room noticed the sudden feverish stare in Joey's eyes. He was still singing. He was still holding the girl. His right hand clutched at her arm. His left hand moved down and over her hips. Still he sang and grinned, but now his eyes seemed blank with terror. The girl tried to wiggle away but his fingers dug into her arm.

Camera 2 panned to the dogs and stayed there.

Blinking, Joey saw the small red light was off him. He released the girl and finished the number, never once having lost a beat.

The commercial came on as soon as the scene was done. Joey staggered to the wings and the valet put a robe around his shoulders. He breathed with effort, trying frantically to remember what he'd done wrong on stage.

The producer was bounding up to him, but he wheeled around and clumped to his dressing room, dragging the valet with him. He locked the door and leaned against it. Jack Gallagher was calling, "Joey! You all right?" He blinked again and pulled the lapels of his robe up to his sweating neck.

"Yeah, yeah, yeah," he answered. "Go 'way, Jack. Gotta fix up for the finale."

"Joey, if you're sick—"

"I said get out, Jack! I'm straight, I'm O.K. Beat it!" And to the valet, "What's next? What's next?"

"Finale. Blue suit."

"Well, get it, get it! Goddamnit, gotta hurry! No time! Gotta hurry!"

His two minutes and eight seconds before the sign-off were successful. He sang his closing number and reminded his audience to donate blood to the Red Cross, and when he finished he received his usual vigorous applause. He hurried back to his dressing room and again he locked the door. Through it Gallagher said worriedly that the Old Man wanted to see him.

"Tomorra!" Joey replied. "Tell 'im tomorra, Jack. I don't feel tops right now. Gonna go home an' sleep, O.K? Say tomorra. I'll be great."

He instructed the valet to check outside. He was told the exit was clear and he walked out, looking straight ahead, answering no one, looking at no one. He raced past the cluster of fans near his car. He jumped in and muttered to Herb, "Home, home, home." He sat back and tried to relax, but he could feel each nerve in his body.

He insisted that Herb come up to the apartment with him. He phoned Dr. Haskill's home and was told the doctor was away for a convention. He swore at the woman on the phone and shouted for Herb. "There's a doc somewheres in the house! Find 'im, find 'im. Tell 'im to come right up! Get out, find 'im!"

Alone, he paced about the entire apartment, switching on lights. He tugged at his necktie and pulled it off. He went back to the kitchen and opened the refrigerator for a bottle of milk. He took the bottle out and it fell loudly to the floor. He started in terror. He slammed the refrigerator door shut and hastened to the bar in the living room. He lifted a bottle of bourbon but he didn't have the strength to uncap it. He ran to the study and searched feverishly for Jean Bixby's number. He called her and demanded, "'Mover here, keep me com'ny. Right away!" He thought suddenly of the Mexican girl he'd known a month ago and, muttering, "Dominga, Domingo, Dominguez ... " he found her number. He phoned her and pleaded, "Please c'mover! Now! 'Mon over, baby! Needja, baby!"

The doorbell was ringing as he hovered over the livingroom bar. Herb escorted a tall and portly man who said his name was Dr. Dodds.

He was saying something, Joey knew, as he submitted to the pricking injection of a sedative; the doc was saying something about nerves and overwork and a bunch of calm and screwy words. And he was answering something. But then he was wearing pajamas and lying in bed and Clyde was nearby and he was feeling better.

The sun was coming through the windows and the clock read twenty-five of twelve.

He sat up and stretched. The hell with last night, he thought, I'm still in one piece. I feel O.K. The doc really knocked it out of me. I feel fine. Hell with last night. I just had a case of nerves, like he said. Overwork.

Rose came into the room with a tray. "Morning," she said.

Joey scratched his chest and grinned. "What's all this special service, doll face?"

Rose set the breakfast on his lap and said, "Doctor's orders. You're to stay in bed all day and I'm to tell him right the second you get up. You're not supposed to move all day."

Joey laughed and he stretched again. "O.K., nurse. That's the best idea anybody's brought me all year. Will do."

Rose stood back as though trying to remember something. "Oh, yes. Telephone. There's a man calls himself Mr. Peck or somep'n. He's on the line; says it's very important."

Joey shook his head and reached for his coffee. "Tell 'im I went to school."

"All right, but he says it's important."

"O.K.," Joey said amiably, and lifted the receiver. "Which button?"

"Two." She went out of the room.

"Yeah?" Joey said.

The man's voice had a creamy quality that irritated Joey. "*Good* morning, Mr. French. I'm George Peague of Peague and Fletcherson. You seem to be a very busy man."

"Peague—what's that, a booking agency? I don't take—"

"Oh, no, no." Mr. Peague chuckled. "It's Peague and Fletcherson, attorneys at law."

"So?"

"I represent Miss Virginia Hutch, Mr. French. I have a statement before me signed by Dr. Hugh M. Grandwaller. In it he states that he has examined Miss Hutch and has found her to be pregnant."

Joey sat up and stared at the breakfast on the floor,

"You are the putative father, Mr. French," Peague said pleasantly. "I would suggest that, in your best interests, we meet at my office for a chat."

CHAPTER TWELVE

IT WAS A FEW MINUTES before two. Al took his eyes from his brother and watched the sun patches on the study floor.

Joey paced the length of the study and fingered an unlit cigar. From time to time he would look at Al and then look instantly away. Al waited. He had been called out of conference with Talbert of the Talbert Music Company—the clerk at his hotel had given Talbert's number to Joey—and been told to come right over. Now he waited, giving Joe a chance to organize his thoughts.

"You makin' out O.K., kid?" Joey asked finally.

"Talbert's giving me a binder on one of my old ballads. He has a record date lined up for it next week."

"Great, great! So you're makin' it with the songs after all, huh? I know Oscar Talbert. Maybe I can put in a word for ya."

"Why did you call me over, Joe?"

"I'll give ya a knife, Al. Stab me for clippin' ya the other night."

Al frowned and lifted his cup of coffee.

"Listen to me, Joe. I know you in and out. What's biting you?"

Joey smiled faintly. "It's a riot, ya know? You come to town on your heels and I'm the king. Now you're ridin' high an' I'm on the ground."

"What is it, Joe?"

Joe dropped his eyes. Then, quite simply, he said, "The Hutch kid."

Instinctively Al sat up. "Oh, Joe!"

Joey's voice lowered but anxiety was alive in his words. "Some guy, calls himself an attorney, gives me the needle on the phone. They figure the name French, that means Fort Knox. Who the hell's got money? Securities, bonds I got. Who's got money?"

"This happened this morning?"

"Yeah. And I'm not in enough trouble. The Old Man's raisin' hell, Bucky Ahearne calls me, tells me I'm in Dutch for carryin' on a little on the show. That I can straighten out, but—"

"The show? I didn't see it. Wha—"

He waved his hand in annoyance. "Nothin', nothin'. I'm in great shape, I can rule the roost till cops an' lawyers an' doctors and those guys climb on my back. Then I freeze. Now she gets herself in trouble an' she gets with this lawyer an' they put skulls together an' dope out how they bleed old Santa Claus so she can retire."

"Maybe it's a trick."

"Ahh, that kind o' tramp, they don't play tricks. One syllable of this leakin' out an' I'm done. But I'm damned if I'm gonna start pourin' out loot. Ya do that once an' they take ya for everything ya got."

There was nothing now to indicate that anything had happened between them. Al said gravely, "There's only one thing to do, Joe. Fight it."

Joey made a noise through his teeth. "Fight it. How do ya fight a thing like that when they're all ready to yell it from the housetops? Haven tells me not to fight it. Give in, he says, give her some dough. Who knows what's right?"

"Haven? You told Haven?"

"Awright, I know there's no love lost between you two."

Al stood and set his cup down. "What in God's name got into you, Joe? You spread news like this to scum like Haven?"

"Ahh, you don't understand."

"Maybe I don't. What goes on between you two? I saw him flying around in the other room when I came in. What is it, Joe, what's he doing in your lap? If I can help at all I've got to know—"

"Help? How can you help? What can you do for me? And keep your voice down." Anger flushed in him as if he had once more been betrayed.

"Then what am I doing here?"

"Yeah, what're you doin' here? That's my whole trouble; I go for advice to crumbs who can't do anything but talk. You got your cool ways about you. I thought you might want to help your brother when he's—"

"Sit down, Joe. And stop it."

The fire raged and Joe glared at him. "Who the hell do you think you are, anyway, that you can sit there an' give *me* advice? I'm on top, but you always get what you go after. I got the success, but you got the health. You haven't got three bucks to your name an' all the chicks with class, chicks that *mean* somep'n, they fall all over *you*, huh?"

"Joe, make sense."

Suddenly the tremors revived in Joey and he shivered help-lessly. "Get outta here, you two-timin' rat! Go back to your classy dames and tell 'em how Joey's messed up, but you're God. Go on, put it in the paper!"

Al started for him, prepared to be hit and to hit back if neces-sary, determined to show his brother that he loved him and cared about him and understood his agony.

He advanced, but Joey backed away, then wheeled and opened the door.

Don Haven, in the hall, looked startled.

"Uh—Joey, I was just—"

Joey walked by him, wordless.

There was no point now, Al knew, in following Joe, in try-ing to talk this out. He stood still until his breath came more evenly.

"Little chat, you two?" Haven still leaned in the doorway.

For a moment Al did not move. When he spoke his voice came slowly.

"Why don't you clear out, Haven? Nothing you can do for Joe is any good."

"Aren't we Humphrey Bogart today?"

Even before he did it, Al knew it was foolish. But his hand shot out anyway, and he wrenched Haven to him by the collar.

"Write this down and memorize it, Haven, you diseased punk: You cause that man any grief at all, and I'll slaughter you."

"Get your filthy hands off me! I'll let Joey know you—"

Al cursed himself for what he could not restrain himself from doing. His fist cracked into Haven's nose, and he heard a sharp, rasping noise as Haven fell against the desk.

Blankly Al looked at the two phone messages from Lory. He moved around his hotel room restlessly, seething at his uselessness. He had called Bucky Ahearne, but the secretary had said Mr. Ahearne was in conference and couldn't possibly be disturbed.

The phone rang and he hurried to it, hoping it might be Joe, or anyone who was a link to normality.

Lory's velvet voice admonished him. "Alan, why didn't you call? I've been so anxious to hear how you did with the song."

"I sold it."

"Well, how modest and unassuming! Darling, we've got to celebrate. I—"

"Lory, Joe's in trouble."

"What is it?"

"Is there any way you know how I could contact the Hutch girl without going to Joe? I don't see her name in the phone book and I can't remember where the hell her father lives."

"Alan, I'm sorry, I don't know. But what is it?"

"Who would know? Who could tell me?"

"Margot Connell, maybe?" Lory offered. "She knows where everyone lives."

"And she's not in the book, either. Or Colter. Do you know her number?"

"Oh, damn!" She paused a moment. "There was that note from her, the invitation to the party. I tore it up. Alan, come over. Or let me come to you. I've got to know what's happening."

Al looked at his watch. A little past four. "Darling, I have to try to settle something. I don't want to go into it on the phone. Will you wait there until I call back?"

"Of course, Alan, but—"

Suddenly time was running out, slipping by before Al could do something, anything. He said good-by, hung up, and flipped through the phone book for the number of the Press-Dispatch. He called there and asked for Miss Connell. He was told she was not in and someone suggested he write a letter. He asked for her home phone, saying it was an emergency, and was refused.

It occurred to him that Clyde Waverley might know. He called Joey's place. No answer.

He called Bucky again. He was asked to leave his number.

The telephone rang as he was reaching for his coat, with only a vague idea of where he was going. It was Clyde Waverley. His voice was urgent.

"Will you meet me in, say, half an hour, Al? It's important."

"About Joe? What is it, Clyde?"

"Not over the phone. I'm getting a cab now. Where do you say? Astor mezzanine? Any place where we can talk."

"What about here? Come up to my room."

"Yeah, good. Let's have that address again."

Clyde appeared at a quarter of five, drawn and defeated. "Got a drink in the place?"

Al handed him a bottle and glass, and saw his hands shake. "What is it, Clyde? Come on."

"I just got kicked out. Fired. Thrown out of the apartment. I don't know what's happening. He's out of his head."

"Joe? What is it? What's *happened,* Clyde?"

Clyde examined the bottle, marking time, collecting his thoughts. "I told you I've seen him in every condition," he began quietly. "But since he began palling around with Haven, he's—I don't know, Al—he's a completely different guy. One minute he's shouting at him and the next minute he's listening as if Haven's preaching the original Sermon on the Mount. Haven's the only one he lets into the apartment these days, except you this afternoon, and me. And it's been that way for the past few days, Al. Strange, crazy stuff. He's starting to drink heavily. And Joey rarely drank."

"Why did he fire you?"

Clyde looked at him squarely for the first time. "Listen to me, Al, and stay calm, because frankly, I'm scared out of my wits." He took a deep breath. "Al, they're talking about a murder."

"A—"

Clyde nodded. "Like two kids playing at conspiracy. I heard only snatches at odd times. Planning to get rid of her. Her, her; I don't know who they mean. The Kimball girl? Ginny Hutch?"

"You're sure about this, Clyde?"

"Do you think I'd make it up? It started with Haven, I'm sure of that. He's been putting ideas into Joey's head about how things would be so much better if she were out of the way, how he can take care of everything. Joey fights back once in a while, but then he gives in and agrees with Haven. I could only catch a word here and a word there, enough to give me a feeling that something's being hatched. Then Joey caught me listening at the door about an hour ago, and he tore the roof off the house. Hit me in the mouth and kicked me out, Al! Told me I'm against him, called me all kinds of names, and made me clear out. He's acting like a lunatic!"

Clyde knew nothing more. Harried, Al questioned him, but learned only enough to amplify his own fears. He phoned Joey again and again and got no answer. He asked Clyde where he could reach Ginny, and wrote down a Queens number. He called there. No answer.

"Where are you going, Al?" Clyde asked.

Al took his coat. "To Queens."

He toyed with a World-Telegram on the train to Queens. There was a quarter-page ad about the Madison Square Garden benefit for tomorrow evening, with Joey French as M.C. He folded the paper and stuffed it into his pocket, unable to concentrate.

A few days ago Joey had boasted about the thirty-seven people whose job it was to look out for him. Where are those thirty-seven people now, Al thought, now when he needs them? Where are the millions of people who wait to see him every week? The character with the innate talent for friendship. Where are the friends? Joey's drowning and there's no one to save him.

You least of all, Al told himself; he gave you the SOS every time you saw him. But you had to be cautious. Things would work out somehow, you said, and now, when the city's ready to crumple on him, you're going into action. What's your plan, big wheel? What are you going to do when you find Ginny Hutch?

It took him twenty minutes, after he'd got off the train, to find the apartment house. The building in which Clement M. Hutch lived was shadowy and spotless and drab.

Al's watch read six-thirty-seven. He heard a phone ring from Hutch's apartment. But no one answered it or admitted him.

He cursed aloud. It was a day burdened with no answers, no solutions. He found the basement and asked the superintendent when Mr. Hutch could be expected home.

"Hutch? Three-G? He come home usual 'bout seven, gentleman."

"What about his daughter?"

The man's mouth turned downward. "I don't know 'bout her. Didn't see her a month, two months." He excused himself and Al returned to 3-G.

A quarter of seven. He walked to the corner and called Joe once more. Still no reply. He called again.

At seven he went back to Hutch's apartment. From the hall he heard the telephone ringing again. At seven-twenty Hutch appeared.

The old man, rumpled and badly shaven, recognized Al immediately as the compassionate man of Nora's party. He came close to Al and stared up in anguish. "She's dead!"

"No, Mr. Hutch," Al soothed, certain that the old man probably knew less than he did. "I was just looking for her. I was in the neighborhood—"

"What is it, mister? Tell me! She all right?"

"I haven't seen her, Mr. Hutch. Now calm yourself."

Hutch unlocked the door, all the while searching Al's face for clues. Al followed him in. He understood a part of Ginny's frustration. It was a dark apartment, littered with overstuffed furniture that bulked at you wherever you turned.

"Please, mister. Tell me why you come. Virginia was here yesterday, says how she's goin' to Mexico for a job. You know about that, mister? You in this theatre business?"

"Uh—yes, that's right. I just wanted to check to see if she was definite about it."

Hutch wandered around chairs and tables, still in his overcoat, looking lost among his own possessions. Al watched as the old man shuffled to the mantel. There were four photographs of Ginny, each framed, in various stages of development. What Al thought must be the most recent one was a bit startling. She wore no make-up and she smiled sweetly. Her adolescent prettiness was evident. This was the Virginia the old man knew and loved and worried about.

"Didn't you say you knew Joe France, the actor, mister?"

"Why, I— That's right," Al said. "I'm told they're not seeing each other any more, that Virginia's coming along very well on her own. Do you know where I can reach her, Mr. Hutch? I want to make sure she'll have everything she'll need for her trip."

Hutch stared at the photographs, lost in memory. "I don't know anything for the past six months, mister, about my little girl. It's like she woke up one day an' says she's gonna live with the devil. She isn't no bad girl, mister, not really. She just got in with bad folks. Only thing, she wanted to be a big star, ever since she was a baby. Anything big, famous, that she didn't have to work too hard for. Just last night she's in here when I come from work, an' she's packin' a couple things she left behind when she moved out the first time. She's sorta more easygoin' last night. She even kissed me before she left. She says everything's fine an' dandy an' she's gonna be a big star in the moving pictures. Then she—"

The telephone rang.

Al stood back while Hutch shuffled to it and said, "Hello?" Al saw his frown deepen. Apparently the caller was a stranger, an imperious stranger. Hutch cut in weakly with "How's that?" and "I don't understand. Who is this?" He glanced at Al, baffled.

Al moved forward and took the receiver. He heard a man's calm and pleasant voice: "... all day to find you in, Mr. Hutch, but I'm a persistent phoner. You don't know me, as I said. But I know your lovely daughter, Virginia. I've been looking out for her in this wicked town, one might say."

It was Osborne Colter's voice.

"And as a friend, Mr. Hutch, I feel I should be the one to take the responsibility of telling you some unfortunate news, before someone else tells you. The fact of the matter, sir—"

Al made a motion to Hutch that said, It's for me.

"—is that lovely Virginia has been impregnated. By Joey French."

Al's teeth gritted. He mumbled, "Uhh ... " into the phone.

The voice continued: "I know that this is a blatant way to bring you such news, Mr. Hutch, and I apologize for it. But if I can be of any service to you, any help at all, please let me know. I can give you any information you need. Ah—are you there, Mr. Hutch?"

"Uh."

"Would you care to meet me, at your convenience, Mr. Hutch?"

Al's finger depressed the hook. He said, "O.K., thanks a lot, Charlie. I'll see you later." He hung up and turned to the old man. "For me, Mr. Hutch. He mistook you for me. I'm sorry to go now, but I've been called downtown. Will you excuse me?"

"Mister, I don't understand any of—"

"Believe me, Mr. Hutch, there's nothing to worry about. I'm sure of that. I'll talk with you again, all right? Good-by, Mr. Hutch."

Colter's butler explained that Mr. Colter was not at home, nor was he expected. Al brushed past him into the foyer. "Tell him it's French. Alan French."

"But sir, I told you—"

"Alan French. Or do I take the place apart?"

The butler bit his lip and said, "Will you wait one moment, sir? I'll see when he'll be back." He turned to leave, and saw Al just behind him. "If you'll wait here, sir—"

"Let's go," Al said.

He heard Colter's voice answer the butler's knock. "Yes?"

"Sir, there's a Mr.—"

Al opened the door against the butler's protest. Colter sat in semidarkness near a window, his head resting languidly against the back of a red leather armchair, his fingers around a wineglass. One of the Brandenburg concertos drifted from an invisible phonograph. Colter wore a dinner jacket. He was smiling.

"I'm terribly sorry, Mr. Colter," the butler said angrily, "but this—"

Colter was unruffled. "Let me guess."

"I'll save you the trouble. Alan French. Send your boy away, Colter."

"All right, Laurence." Colter waved briefly. Laurence closed the door behind him. "Now, Mr. French. Sit down, won't you? As I recall, you drink Scotch. May I—"

"Sit still." Al tried to restrain his hostility. "What's your gain in hacking away at Joe?"

"I haven't been called a hack, Mr. French, since—"

"Get out of the drawing room and talk! You called Hutch, and God knows what else you've done. What's in it for you, Colter? What's Joe to you? Where do you come in?"

Colter's smile widened. "No hysteria, please. You've been grossly misinformed, young man."

Trembling, Al lunged at him and grabbed his lapels. The glass dropped and broke on the floor. Colter's smile froze.

"What is it, Colter?" Al breathed. "Does blindness give you rights the rest of us don't have? What goes on in that aesthetic, diseased mind of yours?"

"Don't hurt me."

"How many people are you guiding? Haven? Ginny? Why are you doing this? *Why?*"

There was a perceptible pause, and then Colter answered, his voice accusing. "You are protecting him! They're all protecting him! They protect the strong, virile men, never the defenseless ones! Yes, I *hate* virile men who ride roughshod over us. They live as they please and they're encouraged. They find their women indiscriminately, they seduce them, and then they throw them away! I *loathe* them for it!"

"Col—"

"But you protect the strong, don't you? The strong must remain powerful and the weak must be swept into the rubbish. I won't allow that! I won't permit ... " His voice trailed off into a whisper and he struggled to free himself. He was frightened now, the composure broken.

"Laurence!" Colter called.

Al's grip lessened and he felt frustration gnawing within him. "Whatever it is, Colter, you can't win."

"There are times when winning is imperative, young man," Colter said, confidence returning. The door opened. "Laurence, Mr. French was just leaving."

Al released him and stood. "All right, call the watchdogs," he muttered hopelessly. "Call the watchdogs."

Ernie, the elevator operator, said he hadn't seen Joe enter or leave. Al went up and tried to get in. He used his key, but the lock had been changed.

He returned to the lobby and sank into a chair, staring blindly at the Venetian mirror on the opposite wall.

Upstairs Don Haven poured another drink and went over the plan for tomorrow night. Joey nodded. Everything would be so simple.

CHAPTER THIRTEEN

IT WAS RAINING HARD at half past two the next afternoon. Don drew the living-room blinds against the dampness and turned up the floor lamps. Joey phoned the answering service and instructed the woman there to have Miss Hutch call him. He gave his number, but would not leave his name.

He hung up and blinked at Don. Don grinned. Joey went into his bedroom.

He hadn't long to wait. The phone rang sharply within an hour and the piercing sound shocked him. Slowly he moved to it, running damp fingers over it until it rang again.

He lifted the receiver and said gruffly, "Yeah?"

"This is Ginny," she said with hesitance.

Joey was somehow strengthened by her little-girl voice. "You know I been tryin' to get you since 1776? Where you been?"

"Where've *I* been? You making jokes again?"

"Who's jokin'? Baby, what's the idea you run around in the street an' everyplace an' you see everybody but you don't come see me?"

"Then you heard from my lawyer," she said.

"Boy, did I hear from your lawyer! You sure he's a lawyer, baby? He sounds like a comic I knew once in Jersey City."

"Joey, ya wanna hear the truth, I can't figure you out. If you're trying to sweet-talk me or something, then I'm very busy and I can't be bothered to talk."

"I don't know where you get sweet-talk, Gin," Joey said with the beginning of a smile. He pulled a chair to him and sat easily. "I'm tryin' to talk like a gentleman. You don't wanna talk, O.K., you don't wanna. Good-by."

"Wait, Joey!"

"You said you don't wanna talk to me."

"What do you want to talk about?"

"You an' me. But if you got to hang onto that lawyer like some chaperon, what can I say? You're grown up, you know your own mind."

"Who says I have to? I know my own mind. I just want to be protected, Joey. This is a very serious matter."

"So act like my Gin an' trot over here where we can talk. Who wants to talk serious matters over the phone?"

"You mean you really want to talk?"

"You want me to write it out in trigonometry for ya? I'm tellin' you I've been doin' a lot of thinkin'. I wanna discuss. That's all I'm callin' to say."

There was a pause. Joey lit a cigarette.

Finally, "Mr. Peague and I'll be over in, say, an hour."

"Awright, forget the whole thing. Peague I don't need. Good-by."

"Wait, Joey."

"So?"

"You gonna be there in, say, an hour?"

"Half hour."

"I'm calling from uptown. I don't know if I can make it in a—"

"Half hour, Gin, an' I'm ready to act like a right guy. I get outta line once, twice in my life an' you go makin' a whole production out of it. Ninety zillion people in the world I don't understand an' they don't understand me, but you an' I, I thought we knew each other to a T."

Another pause. Then: "Joey . .

"Half hour, baby," he said, and replaced the receiver.

It occurred to him he was clever as hell. He could have pussyfooted at the phone, he could have got sore, he could have stumbled and fumbled. But he'd played the part like he'd never played a part before. He'd known exactly what to say and how to say it. He knew psychology. You don't get to the top of the heap without psychology.

Just wanna get her offa my back, he thought, but people tryna say where I'm tryna do her dirt. I don't do dirt to anybody! Ask anybody! Me a murderer? Where the hell they get off sayin' a thing like that? I wouldn't hurt anybody!

He went into the living room.

Don looked up at him with curious eyes. "My God! I thought a bison was loose in the apartment!"

"Whatta ya mean, bison?"

"That laugh of yours just now. Like a wild animal."

"Me laughin'?"

"Or whatever. Drink, Joey? You'll feel better."

Joey crossed to the bar. Don's presence made him feel stronger, more controlled. He was aware of his eager acceptance of a drink, and fleetingly it annoyed him. He'd seen dozens of show people fold because of the happy water. Good performers, straight, talented, who for some reason or another hadn't been able to go on climbing without a bottle in the suitcase. Joey had made a pledge to himself long ago that he'd always watch his step with the liquor. A drink here and there to be sociable, to relax with a crowd, sure. But at the first sign of tension he would concentrate on ginger ale. But that was —God, so long ago! How long since all those boy-scout pledges were made? No whisky. No women if they interfered with work, with climbing the ladder. No lies, no two-timing, no knives in the back. Live right and you save your health, your name, and you reach the top just as fast. How long since all you needed to keep you clicking were a few quarters in the pocket and somebody's back to slap and a warm bed to sleep in and those good, old-fashioned quilts? How long...

"Joey?"

"Whuh?"

"Do you want this drink, or don't you?"

He blinked. Haven was holding out a glass, a tall one heavy with ice.

Joey took it. "Tell me somep'm."

"Will if I can." Don grinned.

"How come you wear a necktie around your pants instead of a belt like everybody else?"

"The tie? Oh, I don't know. I just never wore a belt. No reason."

Don reddened as Joey continued to study him with almost an idiot blankness. He turned his back and went to the sofa with his own drink. "Uh—did you talk with her? Is she coming over?"

Joey merely stood and focused his stare. Don sat back and crossed his legs, feigning relaxation.

"Joey, what *are* you staring at?"

"You're cool's a cucumber, aren't ya?"

"Cool?"

"Tell me somep'm, Haven. How come you're like you are?"

Don's hands trembled, more in fear than in anger. He put his glass down carefully.

"I ast you a *question!*"

"Listen to me, Joey. I'm not mud. I'm in something with you and I've agreed to take far greater risks than you merely to pro-tect you, so please don't talk to me as if you picked me up out of a gutter somwh—"

Joey advanced slowly. "You gonna answer a man when he asts ya a *question?*"

Haven felt Joey's nearness, and the strange, dangerous mood.

"You not gonna answer a man's *question?*"

"What ... what's the question?"

"Where do you get off actin' like such a cool cucumber? You got nothin' inside ya? You gonna *kill* somebody an' you actin' like you're onna way to a party. Huh? *Answer* me, you lousy—"

Don leaped from the sofa as he saw the glass lifting above Joey's head.

"Joey, God in heaven, put that down! Please, Joey! Sit down. You're on edge, Joey. Relax."

"You gonna do like I say?"

"Whatever you say, Joey. We agreed to that."

"You said about how you're gonna anchor her, throw her over the boat, all that stuff. No! I say no! You don't kill that kid! You don't kill nobody!"

"Last night you said—"

"I never said a word! *You* were the one, puttin' in my head about kill, murder, throw 'er in the lake! I said get her outta the way, I didn't say *kill!*"

"Whatever you say, Joey. Whatever you say. Only sit down, Joey."

"All *your* idea!"

"Please sit down, Joey."

Joey retreated, staring numbly at his glass. Energy had left him and once more he was quiet. Don took a tentative step toward the landing.

"I'll go home now, Joey. You call me when—"

"Sit down," Joey said.

Don sat. "Maybe you want to call this off, Joey."

"You'd kill your mother to get on the show. Didn't you say that?"

Don was silent.

"Where'd you get off, thinkin' I'd say to kill her?"

"Last night you listened to me, Joey. You listened to me plan the entire thing. You agreed it would be the simplest—"

"I didn't say kill."

"Then out of the way."

"I said outta the way. Get 'er off my neck. I didn't say kill. I'll break your head, you say I said kill!"

"All right, Joey."

"So you'll sit an' you'll wait. When I tell ya, then you'll do what I say. What time's it?"

"Nearly three."

"Awright, she'll be here soon. Now go over it again, step by step. Whatta you do when ya get her up there? Step by step."

And as he tried to listen, as he lowered his head and stared at the expensive rug, the thought of murder came once more to appall him. Makin' me out a killer! he thought in horror. I don't kill nobody. Hell, I gave ten grand to the Heart Fund! I make 'em live! Me kill?

He had drained his fourth drink by the time he heard the elevator door outside. He felt wonderfully sober.

He motioned for Haven to go into the study and wait to be called. Haven nodded and went out.

Again he heard the doorbell. He had invented an unusual laugh within the past few minutes, and that had pleased him and challenged him to perfect it. He tried it again as he bounded happily to the door. He asked who it was and heard her voice.

"Hello, Joey," she said, looking at him with large clear eyes. She did not move.

He took her arm gently and guided her in. "What's it, rainin' out?"

"Raining? On and off. Why?"

He shook his head, dismissing the urge to tell her she looked beat up. Her coat was wrinkled and her beret sat limply on her head.

He closed the door and faced her. She stood waiting, like a child prepared for punishment. He embraced her in a mammoth hug.

"Joey, now quit."

"I'm actin' like a nut since ya went outta here, kid. What the hell's the matter with me, I can't get ya outta my system? It's like I'm livin' half a life."

"You sure didn't act it."

"Kiss me that special way, baby. The way that makes my ears fall off."

"Oh, Joey, if I could only be—"

He rocked her back and forth, holding her tenderly.

"Joey ... " she whispered, and put her cheek against his chest.

"Whatta you wanna gimme trouble for, Gin?"

"You know I'm not like that, Joey. But there's this— this matter. An' I got scared. An' I thought you were tellin' me to cut out."

"See?" he said softly, and rubbed his palm over her head. "Shows all you know. What am I, a bum, that I'd run out on ya? It's like I told ya, baby: The whole business don't mean a dime if I don't have somebody to love me back."

"Joey, that's true. About the baby, I mean. I mean that wasn't something somebody went and made up, Joey. I was scared."

"You scared now?"

"I don't want to be."

"Let's take the Eighth Avenue Express to the living room."

Arm around her, he walked her to the front room. He grinned inwardly. He couldn't remember ever having felt so assured. *This* he was going to get serious about? *This* he'd risk a career for?

"You've been drinkin', Joey."

"A little. How'd ya know?"

"I tasted it when you kissed me. I worked up a thirst."

"For another kiss?"

"For a drink, crazy!"

"O.K., but each drink costs one kiss."

They kissed again and he released her to go to the bar. He watched her slip out of her orange coat and sink to the armchair nearest him. The fear had left her eyes and she was watching his every move with a partially hidden adoration.

"Gin an' tonic, keerect?" he said.

"You always used to say, 'Gin for Gin.' "

"That's right. Uh—I know a doc who lives in the Heights, kid."

He took a minute longer than he needed to mix the drinks. He turned to her, grinning innocently, and gave her a glass. She was still looking at him, but adoration had dissolved into bewilderment.

"Joey, you know I'd never do a thing like that."

"Like what? C'mon, Maude Adams, don't make like an actress. I'm only talkin'."

"Well, talk different, then, 'cause I wouldn't in a million years go through a thing like that."

"Awright, I was only talkin'. Here, drink up."

"I don't dig you, Joey, that you'd even say such a thing like that. Mr. Peague warned me you might an' I told him—"

"You bringin that muzzier in again? Whatta we need with Peague? I'm tellin' ya, baby. I'm barin' my chest. Whatever you say, I'll do. Whadda you want from me?"

"I want us to get married, Joey. And we'll forget all of those hassels and stuff. I shouldn't of acted like I did, but I apologize. I love you, Joey, an' I want us to get married an' settle down an' live nice."

"So what'm I, arguin'? I wouldn't let you lose the kid, anyway. Hell, he's my kid. I want a kid, why not? So 1 was talkin'. So we'll just run down to City Hall an' sign the papers."

Ginny sat up, eyes alight.

"Joey, you mean it?"

He chuckled. "What'm I gonna do, say a word like City Hall if I don't mean business? A man doesn't say that unless he means business."

She was kissing him furiously now and he laughed, enjoying it. "Oh, Joey!" she cried. "I love you!"

"Awright, awright. So when the kid comes before time, we'll just say we eloped. Who has to know, right?"

"Oh, *anything,* Joey! I'm just so—"

He snapped his fingers. "Listen! I just got a great idea!"

"What, Joey?"

"You never saw my place up in Garland, did ya? Got a cottage up there with a garden an' sand an' the ocean. You didn't know I was a country boy at heart, did ya? Boy, what an idea!"

"What, Joey?"

"Aw, but you'd need time to pack. No, forget it."

"You crazy? What is it?"

"I was gonna suggest we take a run up there tonight to cement the deal, like they say. But it wouldn't look right."

"To who, Joey? Who cares? I'm dying to go! But I read in the Mirror where you have this here benefit for charity tonight."

Again he snapped his fingers. He got up, finished his drink, and started to make another one. "Damn, that's right. You know what you're doin' to me, kid? I got all these ideas but you're makin' me like I'm ashamed to even look at ya, with your lawyer friend an' your court orders an' all. I got plans but I guess I maybe better prove myself to you first, huh?"

She was up, too, and her arms encircled his waist as he puttered at the bar. He smiled. He was giving the performance of his life, and his only sorrow was that there was no one to whom he could describe it later.

"Joey, you're just like a little kid, you know that? You're so cute. I'd do whatever you'd tell me."

"Well, do you wanna try Garland tonight an', say, tomorrow? I can skip rehearsals for a day. I just feel like relaxin' for a while, especially now I'm gonna wear a ball an' chain."

"You won't wear that. I'll let you have a night out with the boys every week, but no girls."

"I'm tellin' ya, Gin, I'm gettin' excited about the kid. An' *you* havin' the kid. We'll name 'im Abercrombie if he's a boy an' Fitch if he's a girl."

She laughed excitedly. Joey felt a hot bead of sweat drop to his lip. He finished mixing his drink.

He turned to her. My God, he thought, what'm I tryna do here? With plots an' plans an' killin' an' ... an' murder? What can they do me? What can anybody do me? What am I, a killer or somep'm? I don't— I never— Hell, I give ten grand to the Heart Fund an' me they call a killer?

Adoration set in again and Ginny breathed, "Mrs. Joey French!"

"So whatta we horsin' around for? You know Don Haven, don't ya? He's in the study, hangin' around. Whaddaya say I let him take the Jaguar an' he'll drive ya up to Garland? Lemme make a big entrance at about twelve; I can get away by nine-thirty or so from the Garden. O.K., kid? Primp the joint up a little. I'll be up with Herb an' he can take Haven back. How's that sound?"

"If you kiss me again."

"An' call the lawyer. Tell 'im to close up shop, you don't need 'im any more. I wanna feel as if I'm gettin' ya on my own, not because you're holdin' a lawyer at my head. That make sense?"

"Sure, sure, Joey. I wouldn't of done it anyways except for—" She stopped abruptly.

"Except for what?" he asked.

"Nothing, Joey. What should I do, just phone him?"

"What were you gonna say? Except for what?"

"Mr. Colter told me to do it. It's like I said: I wouldn't of caused you trouble for all the world. But this blind man, Mr. Colter, he was very nice at first, he said I should try to get money out of you for throwing me over, and I don't know, it sounded like sense when he put it into words—he talks that way, comes on very cool and refined —and I said O.K. without thinking and he says where he's gonna take over for me and do my thinking for me 'cause you have a lot of money, is the way he put it, and he wanted to look out for my interests. I shouldn't of listened to him in the first place, Joey, but I—"

"What about this baby stuff? Is that Colter's idea?"

Ginny's eyebrows rose. "Oh, *no,* Joeyl What do you think I am? That was solid on the level. And, well, *listen,* Joey, I felt like how I didn't have a friend in the world and all of a sudden he turns up, so why shouldn't I do like he says? I *mean!*"

"Awright. So?"

"I mean I'm young and pretty and I have talent. I mean does it make sense that where somebody wants to help me and advise me, like, where I should leave myself in the lurch?"

"Awright. Go on."

"So Mr. Colter, he sent me to his doctor and I had this checkup and that's what this Dr. Grandwaller found, and Mr. Colter, he said something about poetry justice, whatever that's supposed to mean. Joey, I don't want to talk about it. The more I talk, I'm ashamed. All I want's to live right and—"

"O.K., awright, baby, shhh. You got this creep's number, Peague? Call 'im an' here's what you say. ... "

Joey looked at his watch. It was five minutes of four. He had prompted her well, he knew. She was doing some expert perform-ing of her own, talking with Peague, telling him he'd get a check for his services and please forget everything because everything was all straightened out. Joey felt fine as he listened. Peague would get his check, forget the whole thing, and go on chasing ambulances. The name Ginny Hutch wouldn't stay in anybody's mind. Her father or aunt or brother or somebody would start missing her in a week or so, but how did that concern Joey? What was the worst that could happen? Maybe somebody would raise a howl, but without Ginny in person, what could anybody prove? Or even accuse? He would work it out. After all, it wasn't as if she was going to be killed or anything. He would see to that. O.K., he'd listened to Haven talk about it, but it didn't cost anything to listen. And he'd told Haven no, no, no! All Haven was supposed to do was to get her out of the way, get her off his back. Joey would work it out. He would have some chick phone Peague or somebody from Pittsburgh or Boston or Miami and make like Ginny and say she was taking a vacation. Hell, it would be simple.

Ginny placed the receiver on its cradle and turned to him.

"Mrs. Joey French," she said.

She came into his arms, and for a moment her warmth made him feel incredibly alive. I never killed in my life. I never did dirt to anybody. Who's callin' me a name? Who's sayin' I'd do a thing like that to this kid or any kid? Anybody at all?

"Every time you say that, you got to kiss me," he said.

In his arms, she breathed, "Joey, we *will* be happy, won't we? I wouldn't hurt you for all the tea in China."

"You set to go, kid? I'll call Don."

"Oh, gee, Joey, I wouldn't be able to make it this quick. I got a million things to do."

"What's to do? Waddaya need?"

"Well, gee, Joey, I've got to get ready, don't I? I can't just go like this. I want to pack a couple things and change my clothes and stuff. How's about a couple of hours or so? Say six o'clock? I want everything to be perfect."

Joey laughed. "Happy, huh, kid?"

She kissed him again. "Oh, Joey, you don't know *how* happy! It's all I ever dreamed about in my whole life! We'll be famous and people'll look up at me and respect me and I'll be Mrs. Joey French!"

He laughed again. "You're O.K., Gin."

"One thing I'd love to do, Joey. Would it be all right?"

"What?"

"Call my father."

"Call— What wouldja do that for?"

"Joey, don't you see? I want him to know. I want to say everything's all right now, I'm going to get married, you're going to marry me. It'll make him happy, Joey."

"No."

"Jo-ey! Why not?"

"Listen, baby. The whole world's gonna know about us soon enough. They'll be writin' us up in the Hong Kong papers. But till I straighten things out, you gotta be like a tomb, ya hear?"

"Well, all right, but—"

"You trust me, don't ya?"

"Oh, *sure,* Joey!"

"Then keep this under your wig. You go get your clothes or whatever an' I'll have Don pick you up at six. Fair enough?"

"O.K. I'm staying at the Bettilou Hotel on West Fortyseventh, near Eighth. Real crumby place."

"We'll get ya outta there in a hurry. No more crumby hotels."

"Can't I call my father, Joey? He's off work till tonight."

"I said no."

"All right."

"C'mere, kid."

He held her tightly. His smile assured her. "I'm flippin', kid. I'm bats about ya. You go on up to the cottage, an' all the while you're waitin', plan the wedding, baby. Make out your guest list an' figure out your gown. I dig ya the most, Gin!"

Don was enraged when he returned to the living room and found her gone. "What were you thinking of?" he barked at Joey, who sat chuckling softly. "She's a hopped-up, idiotic adolescent, Joey. There's no telling what she'll do!"

"I'll tell ya what she'll do," Joey said. "She'll go home singin'. She's a young kid, she's got stars in her eyes. I toldja a thousand times, you leave tilings to me."

Don shrugged.

Suddenly Joey looked up, as if he had just remembered something horrifying. "Wait a minute. What time is it?"

"Little after four."

"Who said somep'm about killin' her?"

"Oh, Joey..."

He rose from the chair and Don moved away cautiously. "Did you say it? Somebody said it. Now listen good. You get her offa my neck, that's all. Nothin' else. You hear me? Nothin' else!"

Don relaxed. He walked to the bar and felt better. For a moment he had thought Joey was going to start swinging again. Joey certainly acts strangely when he's drunk, Don thought. He gets illogical, he can't remember a thing.

"Of course, Joey. Don't worry. Everything's going to be fine."

CHAPTER FOURTEEN

AT FIVE O'CLOCK Lory spoke her Saturday-matinee curtain line. When she came off stage her dresser told her to telephone her home.

In her bedroom, Al brushed his cigarette into an ash tray and looked at the phone, waiting for her to call. Bone tired, he rattled the melting ice in his glass, then rose to fix another drink.

Last night and today had been brutal, he reflected. He had sat in Joe's lobby until a quarter of six in the morning, rising at intervals to bang on Joe's door and to call him on the house phone. Twice Joe had answered: once he had hung up on hearing Al's voice, then he had rattled off, "Hiya, fella, how goes it?" That had been the call in which Al had ordered Joe to open the door, to let him in. Joe, the heart of friendliness, had told him, "Look, sweetheart, you're worried. Whaddya worried for? I'm givin' all the energy to next week's show now an' I just don't wanna see ya. Go to bed, lemme alone, sweetheart." And then the click and Al's frustration began spiraling.

He'd called Dr. Haskill at seven o'clock. Haskill had listened to his explanation, and then had told him to calm down, that he'd known Joey for more than a year and Joey had always had enough sense to call his office when he felt himself going off the track. By eleven he'd located Bucky's home. A maid there had reported that Mr. Ahearne and his family had left twenty minutes before, on their way out of town for the week end.

He'd returned to his hotel then, and dropped exhausted on his bed, sleeping fitfully for a few hours, waking to tell himself that Clyde had heard wrong, that Joe was digging into work, that Joe would behave himself. Joe was irrational sometimes, impulsive, a great kidder, but Joe knew enough to—

Now Al brought his third drink into the living room, wondering if he could have done anything more, wondering if he would be to blame if anything disastrous happened. When the phone rang he leaped for it.

"Alan," Lory said, "I've been trying to reach you since last night."

"Hello, baby. Will you come down here? I'll tell you all about it."

When she got there, when he'd kissed her with unexpected hunger, he told her. Omitting the frills and his own suspicions, he told her the whole story. Her reaction was immediate and deeply concerned.

Somehow it was immensely helpful to be with her, Al realized. Her flipness had disappeared the instant he needed support, and he let her know, as she got together a quick dinner, that he appreciated her. Somehow it helped to hear her say that he had done everything he could, that there was nothing more he could do.

The hours between the matinee and evening performances ran out too quickly. Then at twenty after seven a call came for him from Margot Connell. Her voice was strained as she told him she'd called a half-dozen other places trying to reach him. She asked him to go at once to Gate B of Madison Square Garden.

She was sitting at the wheel of her convertible as Al hurried to the entrance. She called to him and opened the door, and he slid in beside her.

"Al, Joey phoned me," she said quietly. "I'd been away overnight. I just got back to town. You—you were at mv place, you know what Popov's been doing." He nodded and urged her to go on. "Al, what's the whole story? I don't understand completely who—"

"Later, later," he said. "What about Toe?"

"The queerest thing. He called me, he began it as a nice, friendly conversation. He said he was on his way here for the benefit. Then he got—illogical. Disjointed talk, strange talk. He said he was marrying Lory Kimball and he wanted me to be the first to know."

"Go on."

"He said, 'Don't tell anyone. It's a big secret.' He talked about you, Al. He said you were a great pal, that you'd seen how wrong it was to steal his girl and you'd given her up and she'd gone back to him. Al, it's so crazy!"

"Go on, Margot."

"He told me to come here tonight, to be with him, to go along with him and Lory to their wedding. That was all. He kept talking but I couldn't understand anything else. He doesn't drink, he couldn't have been drunk. I tried to find you. He sounded so strange, so far away. What's Joey done, Al? What's wrong?"

Al opened the door and got out. "Let's go. Can we get backstage without any trouble?" He walked quickly around to her side but she had already got out. They went to the stage door, then hurried up the ramp. It was eight-ten and the orchestra was tuning up. Al formed a wordless prayer, understanding the nonsense of the phone call. It was Joe's way of pleading: Stand by, Margot, save me. Watch out for me, don't let anything bad happen to me.

Against the somber beat of the national anthem, which signified the beginning of the show, scores of people were organizing themselves backstage, asking questions, affixing carnations, clearing throats, making jokes. Al saw Joey appear suddenly from a half-hidden door, followed by a clucking dresser. Joey slapped away the dresser's hands and said shrilly, "Lemme alone! I'm all right!" Heads shot up to look at him; he seemed aware that he'd raised his voice at the wrong moment and his eyes slithered over everyone as though to offer apology. He continued to the place assigned him, and stood there straight and unwelcoming.

Al, a dozen feet away, felt the powderkeg tension of his brother's temper.

And then the anthem was finished and Joey's theme sounded. He strolled to the mike, waving gaily over the prolonged applause that greeted him. Al and Margot waited and watched in the wings. Joey acknowledged the response, told a standard gag, and then said, "Let's begin this great show tonight with the Suavellos!" More applause. Joey hurried off as three toothy acrobats cartwheeled on.

Joey's shoulders lowered the instant he escaped the spotlight. He saw Margot and Al and tensed once more. He was sweating freely now, and his lips twitched as he tried to move away from them. Al tried to speak over the Poet and Peasant Overture, but Joey shook his head and buried himself in a sheaf of cue sheets. His foot tapped against the floor, his chin jerked nervously as he bit his lip.

"Joe .. " . Al said.

He looked up viciously and rasped, "Go 'way! Go 'way! Who you pullin' at?" A man dashed up to protest the noise and Joey barked at him, "Shuddup! I'm awright!" He glared at Al again and muttered, "See? Don't get me in Dutch. Don't pull at me!"

And then there was more applause and the acrobats appeared. Someone was touching Joey. Joey looked up dazedly and then started ahead. But then he stopped abruptly and looked at Al as if seeing him for the first time. "Whaddaya doin' here? Who ya spyin' on?"

"You're on, Joe," Al said, pointing to the stage.

"Where's Lory Kimball? How come you didn't bring her here tonight? She's your girl, ain't she? So how come you—"

Someone was entreating now, "Mr. French! You're on! You're on! They're waiting for you!"

Joey dropped his papers, squared his shoulders, and walked with dignity to the mike.

Al heard laughter and turned to face the stage. Joey had just produced a one-liner and he was following it now with a rapid fire of quick, punchy gags. Margot relaxed and whispered to Al, "He'll be all right now. The stage is a sort of Enchanted Cottage to him."

"How long is he supposed to be on?" Al asked a man at his shoulder.

"He agreed to go through the whole evening introducing acts, doing a bit here and there on his own. Why? What's wrong? Look, if he's not in condition, I can run for somebody else to M.C. To tell you the truth, he's been acting funny since he came in. Picked a fight with—"

"—took the *bandage* off my *finger* just today!" Joey was shouting, his voice suddenly raucous. "Boy, did it hurt! Damn wire brassieres!"

The man next to Al winced. "Hell. We *warned* him not to throw those cutie-pie lines in. This is being picked up overseas!"

The man skittered away as Joey broadened his patter, drawing a finger across his throat, directing another man to cut off the overseas pickup. The audience was laughing but worry swam around the authorities backstage. Margot clutched at Al's arm; imperceptibly Joey's routine had moved from its assured, smooth performance to an openly nervous and harsh monologue. He was stamping about the stage, clumping away from the mike, laughing each time he said something vulgar, shouting to make sure his voice would carry.

People were snapping fingers at Joey, fighting to get his attention, to warm him, to induce him to bring on the next act and get off stage.

"Who wantsa try it? Who wants the chance to dance with Joey *French? Uh?* C'mon, *c'mon,* girls. I wouldn't hurtcha! *Uh? Answer* me, somebody, goddamnit!"

A uniformed guard was approaching him, but Joey was raging now, his huge fists clenched, prepared to fight anyone who tried to stop him.

"Come *on,* goddamnit! *C'mon,* girls, who—"

His fist drove wildly into the guard's jaw and the amplifying system exaggerated the sound. "Get th' *hell* outta my *act!*" He hit the guard and pushed him away. A hum of anxiety rose from the audience. Three policemen were racing down the aisles. Joey screamed, "My *act,* god-damnit! *My* act! Get—"

Al ran on stage as Joey, maniacally powerful now, roared and punched at all who came near him. He spat words, shouting them fiercely, vulgar words, profane words. Four men were holding him, trying to subdue him. The amplifier had been switched off but the violence from the stage was terribly audible.

"Lemme *go!*"

He kicked and flailed. He was crying now, fighting them off. A policeman raised a stick and cracked it down on Joey's shoulder. Joey twisted and continued to weep and shout.

"Al! Al! Al!" he roared. "Where's Al? Al!"

They dragged him off stage. Al got to him, pushing through oppressive crowds of curious and stunned show people.

"Al! Al!"

"Joe, I'm here!"

Tears ran from Joey's frightened eyes as he reached for Al with both hands. "Save 'er, Al! Ginny, it's Ginny, gotta save 'er! Up in the cottage, she's with Haven! Save 'er, save 'er, save 'er! Ginny! I didn't mean nothin'! Save 'er, Al! Fa God's sake, save 'er!"

Margot put a hand on Joey's arm. "Garland, Joey? Is it Garland?"

He nodded, a plea in his eyes. "Garland! Go there! Save 'er! Garland!"

Margot said urgently, "Al, I know where it is. Let's go!"

"Save 'er! Oh, my God! Sa—" Joey's hands beat at Al's shoulders and he wept. He continued to sob until he turned his great hand and saw the man standing twenty feet away.

Joey's legs gave way for a fraction of a second. His face went ghostly white. Al turned to see what had terrified Joey.

It was Don Haven.

A new roar erupted from Joey. He broke the hold of the policeman and made for Don, who, in turn, broke for an exit. But Joey caught him.

"You killed 'er! God Almighty, you killed 'er!"

Don tried desperately to free himself. People were advancing on the enraged Joey, worried, soothing, or openly curious, and Don spoke swiftly, keeping his voice low, still fighting to escape.

"No. No, Joey! Listen to me. She didn't show up! She—"

"*Killed* 'er!"

Joey's great fist lifted over his head.

"I swear, Joey! She didn't show up! I looked for her but she didn't come! I came here to tell you."

"God Almighty, you *killed* 'er!" As a policeman reached out to restrain him, Joey's fist drove violently into Don Haven's jaw. Don screamed in pain and fear, but Joey's grip never slackened. Over and over he sent his fist at Don Haven's jaw.

"Joey, stop it!" Al commanded.

"I'll slaughter ya, ya rotten bastid, killin' that poor baby! That poor—"

And once more he punched, this time with all the strength within him. When Al and the policeman were able to drag Joey off, the unconscious Don fell to the floor, his jaw bloody and broken, his face distorted.

Someone shouted, "Ambulance!" Near the stage, Joey French went limp.

"Save 'er," he whispered.

CHAPTER FIFTEEN

THUNDER CRASHED over the wet streets past Eighth Avenue, and after it came the high winds and the torrents of rain.

Al hunched forward over the wheel and set the wind-shield wipers in motion. Between him and Margot sat Joey, now muttering, now snoring lightly. Joey's head rested on Margot's shoulder and her left arm drew him closer.

"He's like … a child," she said quietly.

Thank God for the few cool heads, Al thought; for Margot's remembering to tell somebody to phone Dr. Haskill; for both of us able to placate everyone, for getting them to help us take him to the car. The apartment house would be jammed, probably; the news of the Great One's fall would be all over town by now. Police, reporters, the meddlers, the curious—they would all be there. What faced Joe now were silent white walls, barriers to deaden the sounds of life outside. But until then, Al told himself, he's got a right to be protected from the hordes. He's got to know he's protected.

"—gonna be good," Joey mumbled, unmoving. Margot and Al looked at him; these were the first articulate words he had said in the ten minutes they had been driving.

He was docile as he rubbed his cheek against Margot's shoulder and went back to sleep. Al felt a sudden tightening in his throat and wished they were already in the apartment, that Dr. Haskill had taken over, had told them it wasn't so fearsome as they had imagined, that this was simply a temporary breakdown, that … But the image of white walls returned again to cut into Al.

He peered at the street sign. It would take them another ten minutes, at least, to get to the apartment. Within a minute after they had begun to ride, he had told Margot the bits of his knowledge of Ginny and Haven and Colter, as if talk could keep tragedy at bay. Now he asked her to fill in.

"Did you know Colter was out to destroy Joe?"

"Somewhere, somewhere unconsciously, I suppose I must have known," she said, "Poppy was difficult before he lost his sight. When his blindness was confirmed, it may have put the wheels in motion. He set his guns on Joey. You … you recognized some of that on the train. I thought it was just talk, but somewhere I must have known—"

"Why Joe?" Al interrupted.

Her answer was not immediate. "Poppy knew we were friends," she said, never taking her eyes from Joey. "We'd been friendly for a long time. I suppose—"

"You and Joe were lovers."

Margot was silent.

"My guess is that it was some time ago, before Joe began on his merry-go-round. Colter knew it, or sensed it, and concentrated on him."

She did not answer for a while. Then, her voice low and grave in the moving car, she said, "It was in 1945. I was doing radio news for the Dispatch then and I met Joey. He was on one of the network shows, making something like thirty dollars a week. But there was something about him, something—primitive. Perhaps I was attracted to him because he was so very nice to me. I wasn't very beautiful, ever. I came from a good family. Philadelphia. I made my debut in Philadelphia, but I was plain and thin as a string. Then I got engaged to Poppy. I thought I'd never get married, so I got engaged to him. Our wedding was set. Right after that I met Joey. Exciting, basic Joey." She paused for a minute, as if to marshal her memories. "He kissed me. I hadn't had any experience. He … he made love to me.

"We were together for three weeks and two days," she went on, her voice suddenly drained of emotion. "And when it was over I could still live. I could still see him in rooms and endure it. It was as though all the good in my life had been crowded into those three weeks and two days and I could cherish the memory of it.

"I never told any of this to Poppy, but he knew. He always knew. Any man was a threat to him. He married me, anyway. Not with love, though. With hatred."

Al glanced at her.

She caught his glance and smiled thinly. "Sound fantastic?" She nodded. "Yes, but wounded people can do fantastic things." She looked at Joey again. "Joey was something to live for. Just knowing him, just knowing we could meet for a drink or I could give him advice or introduce him to spectacular women like Lory Kimball; just knowing I was part of him was enough for me."

Margot continued to. talk, and part of Al listened. But the likeness of Lory had returned and his fingers gripped a little more securely on the steering wheel as he remembered that Lory was his, that her spontaneity and off-beat beauty and devotion were his. He and Lory might not escape unscathed from this tragedy, but they would stand together, always.

They pulled up at the back entrance of Joey's building. A moment after he turned off the motor, Joey moved forward.

"Where? Whuh ... "

Margot took his hand. "We're home, Joey."

"She awright? The kid awright?"

"All right, Joey. We're home now."

They entered by way of the basement service door. The elevator operator, taking them up, said that the lobby was filled with reporters, all trying to get information.

"No one's to go up to the apartment," Al said. "Is that clear?"

The operator nodded. "Right. Ernie on the front elevator knows, too. Nobody goes up. Only one he let in was the doctor, whatzisname, just a couple minutes ago." He was struggling to keep his eyes away from Joey; his attempts were unsuccessful.

Joey, placid, appeared to understand everything that was happening. He grinned at the operator. "H'are ya? Herman, isn't it?"

Herman touched his cap. "Herman's right, Mr. French."

"How's the wife? Still got arthritis?"

"That's Ernie's wife with arthritis, Mr. French. Front elevator."

"Yeah. I told ya a milion times, ya stubborn jerk, I'll give ya a thousand bucks, take the missus to Warm Springs."

"O.K., Mr. French."

"Don't forget, now."

The maid, Gladys, had the service door open, waiting for them as they came out of the elevator. Joey greeted her, gently freeing himself from Al, and Gladys' chubby hands went out to him. Like an obedient child he moved to her and let her take his arm.

"H'are ya, Gladys?"

Joey seemed fascinated by Gladys' concern. She was restraining tears. As if in response, he grinned a little more widely, still assuring everyone who watched him that he was subdued and well behaved now.

Al slid his hand under Joey's other arm and helped guide him into the apartment. Joey freed himself again and asked, "How long's your husband gone now, Gladys?"

"Fourteen years, Mr. French. Let's take you into your room now. I took out them blue pajamas you like." She looked at Al. "The doctor's in the bedroom."

"Husband was a machinist, wasn't he? Had somep'm wrong with his liver?"

She nodded. Dr. Haskill approached them from another room. Joey saw him but pretended his conversation with Gladys was of paramount importance. "He left a good woman, Gladys." Cautiously he faced Dr. Haskill. "This Gladys is a hunnerd per cent tops, Doc."

Haskill motioned for Margot and Al to move away. "Hello, Joey."

"I'm in kinda bum shape, Doc." Joey smiled. "Maybe I need a li'l rest, huh? Ya think?"

"We all need rest once in a while, Joey. Let's go into the bedroom."

"You figure a week or two for me? I can lay in the sun, get brown. Maybe try Miami or Cuba or someplace like that."

"Let's go in, Joey."

He turned his head to Al and asked with affection, "You stick around, Al?"

"Sure, Joe."

He saw the doctor's hands on his arm. He paused and looked at his hands. "You wouldn't think a big gorilla like me would have such small fingers, would ya?" he said. "I bet two million times my mother said to me when I was a kid, 'Joseph,' she says, 'you have to stop crackin' your knuckles or those fingers are gonna grow crooked.' She said that a hunnerd times if she said it once. Lemme lay down a while."

Al paced the living-room floor and occasionally heard the sympathetic words that Margot offered. When Gladys entered the room, unashamedly weeping, Al felt his own eyes cloud with tears.

"He's givin' him one o' them needles in th' arm," Gladys said, and perched on the edge of a chair. "He's a good man, that Mr. French. He's really a good man. Does he have to go to one of those … those homes?"

"How did you get in, Gladys?" Al asked. "Weren't the locks changed?"

She nodded. "The locks was changed, yes. I been here maybe on hour. I was scared, couldn't tell what was wrong. I came like I always do, an' Rose came, too, an' we just couldn't get in with the locks changed on the doors. I had a feelin', a real feelin'. I talked to the elevator boy an' the super an' they didn't have new keys or know what to say. An' then, sure enough, I tried the back door, an' sure enough, it was unlocked! He must of been really havin' things on his mind, poor man. He *never* leaves doors unlocked. You think he'll have to go to a home?"

Al faced Margot. She was white and distraught; until now she had been unable to compose herself. She started to rise. Then they heard the bedroom door close and Dr. Haskill approach.'

The telephone, which had been ringing almost incessantly, rang again. Dr. Haskill frowned and said to Gladys, "Would you get those people off the line and then go in and sit with Mr. French?" Gladys nodded and left the room. He sat in her chair and looked at Al.

"What is it, Doctor?" Al asked.

"He'll sleep. He seemed sedated enough, but I gave him some sodium amytal. And I've already phoned Dr. Murdock and Dr. Snyder. They're on their way over."

"Who are they? Why are they coming?"

"The law says two physicians with psychiatric training must examine the patient to corroborate the doctor's diagnosis."

Margot began, "That means—"

"Before he can be committed."

The word knifed at Al. "Doctor ... "

Dr. Haskill nodded. "I know. But there's no other way."

"What about Miami? Or Cuba? I can take him."

"You know that's foolish talk, Mr. French. He needs treatment."

Once more Margot rose. This time she moved slowly, as if she were abnormally tired, to the end of the living room.

"I'm going, Al."

"Yeah. Thanks for everything, Margot."

"Would you use the back door?" Dr. Haskill asked. "There were dozens of people in the lobby as I came in. There are probably more now. No use fighting through the crowd."

Margot nodded and went out. Al, wanting to ask scores of questions, said nothing.

For a moment there was no sound or movement. Then they heard the rear door open.

The two men looked up. Al wheeled and started for the kitchen.

Mr. Hutch was entering the apartment. There was a gun in his hand. Margot backed away from him.

He looked no different from the times Al had seen him before. There was determination in his eyes, but he was the same troubled and mild little Mr. Hutch.

Except that now he held a gun.

Margot was retreating in terror. Al's hand came up, closed on her arm. Mr. Hutch advanced an inch and shut the door with his foot. Along with the certainty of danger, Al felt a curious rush of pity for the old man. For a while no one spoke. The gun was obviously a foreign instrument to Mr. Hutch, but as he stood before them, weaving in his fear, Al saw the veins standing out in the little man's hand, and somehow this signified strength.

Finally Mr. Hutch spoke. His lips quivered but his voice was surprisingly clear.

"Where is he?"

Al said quietly, "Put that away."

"I said, where is he?"

"Put that down and we'll talk."

Hutch's voice broke, but as if to counteract this, he raised the gun and motioned them all back. "I'll find him. I'll find that man. Get back! Get back, tell me where he is!"

Margot fell against the wall in panic.

"How did you get in?" Al asked.

Mr. Hutch looked beyond him and called to Dr. Haskill, "You! Get him! I know he's here, now get him!" To Al he croaked, "I trusted ya. I see ya an' I trust ya an' you're gonna help my little baby, but you're in with alla them, ain't you? Alla— Mr. Colter told me. Mr. Colter told me everything!"

Margot brought her cold hand against Al's side for support. Al glanced around for Dr. Haskill; he was not there.

Firmly Mr. Hutch inched them back. They heard the bedroom door open and then a peculiar roar from Joey, not of anger or of pain, but a roar of greeting. Al kept his attention on Hutch, who was only briefly rattled by the noise.

"Gonna go *back* to the *show!*" Joey cried happily. The voices of Haskill and Gladys were heard, trying to quiet him. "Feel *good! Feel* marvelous!"

Al talked rapidly. "Mr. Hutch, he's a sick man. Let him alone, let him rest! He's sick."

"Hurt my baby."

"Put that down, Mr. Hutch. He's sick."

Gladys was trying to restrain Joey as he clumped toward the front room. Dr. Haskill, too, was reaching for him, but Joey, alive and laughing, proceeded to where he'd heard voices, as though no gathering could properly continue without him. He wore gay blue pajamas and they matched the merriment in his face. The loud entrance was remarkable to Al; Joey seemed to be saying, No needle's putting me under. As long as I live I'm going to keep the motor running, keep running at the top of my lungs, keep laughing because when I laugh it means I'm strong and I can punch hell out of all the tigers. No needle can stop me. Nothing can stop me.

Ten feet way, the gun rose, aimed at Joey's head.

Al saw Hutch's hand tremble. Joey appeared to notice nothing.

"Hand me down my cane!" Joey laughed. "I'm M.C. tonight!" He continued to laugh, even when he seemed to be fully conscious of the gun. His laughter lessened gradually as he fastened his eyes on Mr. Hutch.

"H'arya?" he called, as if he were trying to place this visitor.

"Make your prayer, Mr. France," Hutch croaked. "You hurt my baby."

Joey, chuckling, glanced at the others. "Who's the fella, huh?"

"God love me!" Mr. Hutch breathed. His index finger closed around the trigger. Al darted forward, blocking Joey, and lunged for the gun.

Hutch fired.

Al heard a scream as he fell. He could see the gun dropping to the floor, and as his body doubled up he could see, before the room and the apartment and the city swam away, the huge figure of his brother Joey running to him, crying out in fear and rage, running, worried, protective.

CHAPTER SIXTEEN

A L LOOKED across the white squareness of the hospital room and his first association was with death.

Then Dr. Haskill was standing near him and he became conscious of weakness and pain. He tried to move, but he felt the constriction of bandages.

Dr. Haskill smiled and said, "Not yet, young man. Just lie still."

"Joe?"

"Joey's all right. He wasn't hurt." Haskill felt his pulse, said something about the bullet that had missed his heart, about his being expected to stay quietly on his back.

Al had dreamed, he knew, and he had been shot, and he had dreamed some more. When had the bullet been taken out? Why couldn't he find the strength to speak, to make a sound?

"—Kimball?" the doctor was saying. "Will you see her? I said she could have five minutes, no more."

And then, within the erratic behavior of time, he saw Lory in Haskill's place. Lory was here.

"Alan . . Her lips were brushing over his eyes, his cheek, his lips.

"Hello, darling."

"Alan, I though—I thought I'd lost you."

"I'm fine, baby."

Gradually Lory composed herself.

"You were unconscious for two days and nights," she said, and held his hand. The news for a moment seemed fantastic to him. He watched Lory. He tried to stay awake, to watch this girl with the yellow hair who was near him, and who loved him.

"—don't know yet what's going to happen to Haven. He's in a hospital with a broken jaw."

"That's good news."

"I talked with Margot yesterday, Alan. She was here, too. She made that detestable husband of hers confess everything. The papers have been working overtime trying to get the story."

He remembered Ginny Hutch now and her name and face appeared before him as if she were a piece of important unfinished business.

"What about the Hutch kid?"

"She's with her father out in—Queens, isn't that where he lives? And from what I gather, she's repenting all over his apartment. And by the way, she is quite definitely not with child."

Al frowned.

"According to Osborne Colter," she went on. "He told Margot it was a hoax. He was concerned with destroying Joey—she wouldn't tell me why—and sometime recently, he and Ginny came together. He had some fifteen-cent doctor make out a pregnancy report and send it to an attorney, and the attorney used it to scare Joey."

"Ginny knew all this?"

Lory nodded. "She figured it was a sort of insurance policy, I suppose. She was going to milk Joey in one way or another, and Osborne Colter was the maestro."

"What about Haven? That Connecticut thing?"

"Colter didn't know anything about that, about ... their planning a murder. The police got it out of Don Haven. Everything had been dandy as far as Ginny was concerned; she thought she'd got her man back. But she phoned Colter to tell him the news, that Joey wanted to take her to the church by way of Connecticut. Colter didn't like giving up that easily. He thought that maybe Joey was serious about marrying her. So he convinced her it would be best for her to clear out of town for the week end and keep them guessing. In his own evil way he prevented a murder."

"Tell me, Lory. The truth, now. Is Joe in good hands?"

"He was taken to Benneford. They'll do wonders for him up there. The important thing now is for you to get strong, darling."

There was time for her to kiss him once more, before the nurse appeared. He turned his head on the pillow to watch Lory go to the door, to see her face, to share this moment's nearness with her.

When she went out, her presence remained in the room, warming Al, and he could face with clarity the thought of Joey. Joey had been defeated that night far more finally than if he had died. The doctors would take some of the ferocious tigers out of his head, but they would be unable to cure his infection of success.

What was there in the climate of success that had rocked Joe? Al wondered. Joe and Ginny Hutch and Osborne Colter and Don Haven? What in hell is this great bubble that they chased with such terror?

He was sleepy again. He and Lory had their own tigers to slay, he knew; together, they might be able to help slay Joey's.

He closed his eyes and waited for Lory's return.

THE END

www.ingramcontent.com/pod-product-compliance
Lightning Source LLC
Chambersburg PA
CBHW052007240626
47153CB00008B/2779